The House on
Parkgate Street

THE HOUSE ON PARKGATE STREET

AND
OTHER DUBLIN STORIES

CHRISTINE DWYER HICKEY

NEW ISLAND

THE HOUSE ON PARKGATE STREET
First published 2013
by New Island
2 Brookside
Dundrum Road
Dublin 14

www.newisland.ie

P/B   ISBN 978-1-84840-290-4
ePub   ISBN 978-1-84840-291-1
mobi   ISBN 978-1-84840-292-8

Cover design by Andrew Brown
Typeset by JVR Creative India
Printed by ScandBoook AB

New Island received financial assistance from
The Arts Council (An Comhairle Ealaíon), Dublin, Ireland

10 9 8 7 6 5 4 3 2 1

IN MEMORY OF BILL

Contents

Across the Excellent Grass

For a while she believed the racecourse was in a different country, so strange it seemed from her own house, just twenty minutes ago. Each suburb passed was a city crossed, each mile a thousand covered. It was as if she'd been on a day out with Mary Poppins and had placed a button-booted foot down on a chalk-drawn scene, watching it melt into the pavement as the picture grew to life about her, making her part of a mystery that was not her own.

And this is how small she was then and always walking with the left arm raised and the left hand held by a power greater than hers, that guided and pulled and shrugged her through the crowds, and coming face to face with nothing except for handbags square and smooth or binoculars, badges bunched swing-swong from their straps. Flutter – 'I have been here'. Flutter – 'I have been there'. And no one to see their gold-cut letters save the child that tagged behind.

And then her head would be skimmed by a dealer's stall, fruit upon fruit laid out on sun-sharpened cobbles. And it could have been the roof of a Catalan house. And it could have been a Spanish voice that cried in words harsh and almost familiar, 'AAAPPLEANORRINGE. OOORINGEANAPPILL …'

And then the arm could come down and wrap itself around her and she would be raised legs loose little stork, eyes squealing at the two bubbled toes of freshly whitened sandals. Flying yet higher for a moment in a soar so glorious. Then swing. And then swoop. And how would they land? Please not on the bars of the iron-cruel turnstile or not so the dust rises over their straps. Veer to the concrete clean and hard and the spark that shoots up through the legs won't matter. Just keep the white white, little stork. Keep the white white.

And then the loud grunt beside her head.

'She's getting big, eh? She's getting big.'

'I'll have to be paying for her soon enough.'

Sometimes the crowd, so sure before, would hesitate and stop and the drum of hooves would come from behind the trees, passing in a string so fast they might be caught in a photograph, so fast no individual movement could be seen.

'Quick. What was the first number you saw?'

And, quick, she would lisp the first number that came into her head, never really able to pick out any one in the streak of saddle and flesh and the long, bright blur of colour mixed.

'What did she say? What did the child say?'

And for once she could be heard and welcome, face puffed pink from her own importance.

'Ah yes. The luck of the child. Number 3, did she say?'

'What's that in the next …? Ah yes. The child brings him luck.'

But he keeps a little black man in the boot of the car for that. Not a full body, just a head and a neck. He said he lost his legs at the Curragh and his hips at Fairyhouse and his arms and his chest at Cheltenham and he could have lost his willy anywhere. Longchamps, maybe Ascot. And once a man sitting in the front of the car had said, 'He wouldn't be the first fella to lose his willy at one of those places.'

Now all the luck was in his head and his brains were in his neck. She said he must have been very small anyway even when he had all his bits and bobs. 'Ah, but you see,' the man in front had said, 'his mother was a pygmy and his father was a jockey and so it was bound to be.'

And now the head as small as a fist came everywhere, an eye on either side and cut like a tadpole and being able to see east and west at the same time. Able to see you no matter which side of the car you were on. And scratches on the pointed chin and across the mushroom nose where the luck had chipped off over the years, and she must chip off even more, graze her hands raw if need be, so important it was to the day. Feeling his hard head on her palm when, after her father, she would rub her hands in rotation, roundy round, and copy the chant that extracted the luck. But she was afraid of him: the little black man that was in charge of the luck. For yet she might see her father's elbows sharp above her move like scissors in the air, and yet she might see fall to her feet the slow, coloured confetti of torn-up dockets drop disappointment on their day.

And she would think of him now, his mean black head stuck in the hole of the spare tyre where she had left him, upside down. How angry he would be. How spiteful, if he chose.

But the horses are past now and the men in grocers' coats flip back on either side leaving a gap for the feet to move through. The crowd begins to spread itself apart leaving spaces where she can see now, the familiar and the wonderful. Here on the right, and penned in by shiny white fence, the ring of careful grass and its outer ring of clay scuffed like brown meringue, where delicate hooves have tipped themselves upward on parade. And here, too, another brim with stool after tiny red stool, the exact amount of space from each to each, and the spongy seat tight clung with artificial leather. But not hers now. Not yet. Now a bottom droops over each one. Later on, when the spots and flowers and the salad and whirls of female colour have taken themselves off, and later on when the men in straw or donkey-brown hats have led the way to celebration or condolences. Then. Then they would be hers, to spin like tops or talk to as a teacher to her pupils. And she can watch them from the seat that travels around the tree amongst the green and the quiet and the dots of dockets, thin as tissue and as useless now. She might eat a bar of chocolate while she waits, square by square and slowly, like the mouth on the television. Or the other one, the one that runs in pyramids down a pale yellow tunnel of paper and foil, the points of chocolate catching on the roof of her mouth at first, then melting into almonds and honey and secret crunchings. So long, it may take all year to eat it. So long.

But that would be later and now is now and her father's thick, warm hand is ever pulling.

First walk up to the little house in the middle that looks like a wooden tent, the one whose floorboards moan beneath the feet, and the woman with the white fluffy hair and the chalky lips, penicillin pink. And waiting. Always waiting for the talk to stop.

Up in the air and only some words heard, 'claiming this and carrying that and ground too this and proved form here and no chance there and Barney Chickle in the long bar says sure fire certainty from the brother's yard and sure fire certainty to lose if that eejit's and ...'

Oh, hurry up. Hurry ... and she grabs the cloth of his trousers making ding-dong bells from the baggy bits behind his knee.

Turns on his heels and nearly knocks her.

'Got to go.'

'Good luck.'

'Yeah. Good luck.'

Now at last outside and there they are. Up above and skirting the balcony, cloaks red and navy hanging across shoulders and more navy in the hats neat as bricks on top of their heads and raising instruments like golden toys from the raw knees squeezed up from woolly socks to pursed lips that push and pull sound into shape for the crowd below. And making a change to the mood too, and the step. The men a little looser at the knee, the women a little heavier at the hip. And *hooop* – a flash of brass stands up and caws and here and there a human hums in recognition. These are the Bold Boys. The boys from Artane. The boys who look no one in the eye unless he too wears a cloak and an instrument. The boys who will come down the wooden steps and march red-necked and eyes down before the off, to point their brass to the sky and herald *den den derrran* ... the horses are coming, they are coming ... here they are.

Oh, what did they do that was so bold? No one tells. Is it as bold as her bold? Is it as great? Could she end in a place where sins are hidden under the fall of a cloak. Could she play music so sweet?

And now turn to the clock standing like a giant's watch with hands so long and spear-tipped pointing at lines. No numbers. Behind it the bushy tails of the Garden Bar peep green through the fence. Women move and stop. Move and stop. Eyeless under brims so wide. Except for lips – pink and orange and red, one rosebud on each plate.

And more knees to greet and more possibilities to be swapped and sometimes stop and, 'My, she's getting big,' and, 'That can't be her – I wouldn't know her, soooo big.' And a child could be a giant before the day is done and a child could wear the watch that is a clock with lines. No numbers. But the child smiles tiny through one eye and dips the other scraping off the trousered leg she knows.

'And do you want to go wee-wee, love?' Mini's rosebud asks, and lowers down a hand with fingers knotted and striped with gold, stretching out nails that have been dipped in blood.

And no one looking down to see her shake her head. No wee-wees.

'Take her, Min, as sure as J she'll want to go in the middle of the race.'

So unfair, big fat lie, she never would. She never did. She can go by herself. Big girl.

'See you in the Weigh-Inn so.'

'Thanks, Min, thanks.'

Then he turns away to Mini's husband, little man, leprechaun face. Used to ride himself before – now he talks his way over every furlong to the post, she heard a woman's voice say.

Min never says a word when they're alone. Just pulls. The trinkets at her wrist tinkle softly. A fruit basket, a star, a moon, two little balls on a chain. Always talks and buys her crippsanorange, crippsanorange, when daddy's there.

Only one woman in the ladies' room looks different. Only one of so many. She wears a dress like a pillowslip with a zip up the front and her hair like a woolly hat pulled down around her ears. She is always busy opening doors and handing out pins, eyes looking slyly through the mirror at big brown pennies drop, drop, dropping into the ashtray.

They line up by the sinks and all their twins line up in the mirrors and all the while pencils and puffs and brushes touching this and that on upturned faces. And silence. Mostly silence. There is nothing to hear but toilets clear their phlegmy throats and tick-tack heels move and stop. Move and stop. And, 'Thank you, Ma'am, thank you,' as the pennies drop.

She hates the smell. The pushy perfume smell, heavy on the air. It makes her want to vomit. She is afraid she'll be too sick for her chocolate. Her eyes sting because of the smell or because she wants to cry. Why? She doesn't know the why.

Mini comes out plucking at her skirt. There is blood on her heels. Min asks the woman for a plaster. She takes out a foot that is big and mushy, blood between heel creases, tough and brown. She spreads the Band-Aid onto the wound. Min doesn't say thank you. Nor does she wash her hands. She puts on more lipstick though and then they leave. Min doesn't notice that she hasn't done her wees.

They walk into garden of the gnomes. Her father sits amongst the furrowed faces of the little men. But they all stand, feet firm and legs in archways like plastic cowboys.

There is no laughter now. Just talk. From earnest mouths that still manage to hang a tipless cigarette from one corner, making it dance with words. Everyone owns dark-brown bottles. Some held, some tilted, some left standing for the light to shine through. Her father points his upside down into a glass. He makes black porter crawl up and leave a tide. Through his lips he sucks the black. *Ahhhh*, and the tide falls down to the bottom of the glass then clings. The little men have funny names. Nipper and Toddy and one called The Pig. The Pig runs messages for her father. Slow winks and wise nods. They pass rolls of money and whisper. He laughs when her father laughs.

This place makes her think of the city at night when it should be dark but is not. The balls of light hang from the ceiling like streetlamps and the crowds shove at each other, unafraid. Her father stands up. He is as tall as the highest shopfront.

'I'll go up so and take a look at this one.'

He fingers through his pocket and takes out a note. He points it at The Pig. 'Get a drink for the lads,' he says. When she looks back she sees The Pig nodding at each one and asking what he'll have, as if the money were his own.

And now up the stairs. She pulls herself by the wooden banisters hand over hand. She must stretch her knees up to her shoulder so as not to delay. The man with the loudest voice calls out across the course. Somewhere outside she can hear the Bold Boys *denden derren* the start. She can see nothing. Only if she droops her head to where feet stand with feet, down step after step. Or if she leans right back and looks up to the inside-out roof that lets in no sky. She is too small, a flower in this forest.

The man with the loudest voice draws one long word out across the course. It is a word with a thousand syllables, screechy and pulled through his nose. The crowd begin to join him muffling out names of place and colour and unlikely title.

She lifts back her head to look for the bird. She knows he is here somewhere, huge and still, his head turned in profile, his wings spanned over painted flames that rise like feathers from his feet. Then she remembers. He is on the other side of the roof, the bit that slopes like a wooden fringe, where he can see the fences bend and the horses roll along the grass.

The woman on the step below her wears bright-red shoes with heels as long as scarlet pencils. She begins to bounce now, her dress flouncing slightly and her feet clicking up and down again. She stops for a moment. She starts again. This time she lifts one foot altogether from the ground. There are scratches on the sole of her shoes and a name in gold that is beginning to fade. Letters from her own name. She shuffles to the edge of the step to take a closer look. The foot starts to come back to the ground, heel first. This time it doesn't return to its own step. This time it pauses in the air and then falls, landing on the step above where her white sandals perch waiting on the edge.

It is like a sword flung from a height onto her toes. She calls out but her voice is silent amongst the urging and the pleading amongst the …

'Go on, ye good thing. Go on.'

She cannot reach for her leg because her foot is trapped beneath the sword. She is pinned to the step by the point of it, stabbed between her big toe and the next toe. She is afraid to move in case the sword slips and cuts off one of her toes. The tears pop out by themselves and roll like rain down a windscreen. A pain pushes down from her stomach and she screams. She knows what is about to happen now. The woman moves her heel away and her foot is free. But it is too late. She lowers her head. She watches the water trickle down the inside of her legs, down, down it goes, staining the hem of her upturned socks. She opens her legs and lets the rest fall down in little splashes, darkening the concrete with its pool.

The roar of the crowd cuts to silence; the last dribble drops. People begin to turn round towards her and start up the steps to the bar at the back. The woman in the red shoes looks at her, then at the pool, then back at her. Her rosebud tightens in disgust.

*

Afterwards she clutches her chocolate like a staff and walks through the crowd to the green outside. She can hear her father laugh loudly behind her. She can hear him change his voice to say, 'Stay on your tree-seat, I'll be out in ten minutes. Good girl.'

She walks on feet she must keep soft and sneaky, laying one before the other as though it were a game. She is unheeded by the stragglers and the dealers. She keeps her head down, watching the frozen splashes on her sandals and the dent so deep that it is almost a hole. Her thighs smack kisses off each other, rubbing the rash that is beginning to rise. Between them she feels her knickers dry hard and crisp, like knives cut into butter.

And in her little head, just for a while, she forgets her name and this place through which she walks. Though somewhere before her she knows there's a little black man waiting to be unstuck. And behind her the Bold Boys are folding instruments silver and gold into themselves and watching her from a height wade slowly away from the wooden house, across the excellent grass.

Absence

The first thing he notices is the silence. He's in the back of a cab, a few minutes out of Dublin airport, on a motorway he doesn't recall; cars to the left and right of him, drivers stiff as dummies inside. And he thinks of the Mumbai expressway: day after day, people hanging out of windows, exchanging complaints or pleading with the sky. The outrage of honking horns. And the way, for all the complaining and head-cracking noise, there is a sense of something being celebrated.

Frank had known not to expect an Indian highway – youngfellas piled on motorbikes and leathery-faced old men wobbling along with the luggage on top of buses – but what he hadn't expected was this. This emptiness.

He has the feeling they may be going in the wrong direction and, when a sign comes up for Ballymun, wonders if the driver could have misheard him. Frank thinks about asking but doesn't want to be the one to break their silence. At the airport there had been a moment, while lifting the luggage in, when a word might have been enough to start up a conversation. But a look had passed between them for a few tired seconds, and somewhere inside that look they'd agreed to leave each other alone.

He'd been expecting the descent through Drumcondra anyhow. Had it all in his head how it would be. The escort of trees on both sides, the black spill of shadow on the road between. There would be the ribbed underbelly of the railway bridge and then, where the light took a sudden lift, a farrago of shop and pub signs running down into Dorset Street. He'd been half looking forward to playing a game of spot-the-changes with himself.

A memory comes into his head then: a day from his childhood, upstairs on the bus with Ma. They were on the way to the airport, not flying anywhere of course, just one of those outings she used to devise as a way to keep them 'off the road' during school holidays. They'd spend the day out there, hanging around, gawking. At the slant of planes through the big observation-lounge windows. Or the destination board blinking out names of places that vaguely recalled half-heeded geography lessons. Or outside the café drooling over the menu where one day, when Susan had demanded to know why they couldn't just go in, Miriam had primly explained, 'Because it's only for the fancy people.'

Miriam loved the fancy people – passengers with hair-dos and matching clothes. Johnny had no time for them. too showy off, he said, flapping their airline tickets all over the place like they thought they were it. And because Johnny had felt that way, Susan and Frank had too. In any case, they preferred to look at the pilots and air hostesses who really were it: striding through the terminal, mysterious bags slung over their shoulders, urgent matters on their minds. Not a hair out of place, as Ma always felt the need to say.

Upstairs on the bus – three kids kneeling up at the long back window. Ma sitting on the small seat behind. In the reflection of the glass her head sort of see-through like a ghost's. He'd kept turning around to check she was still there, with a solid head and real brown hair on top of it. Her hands were in their usual position – right one for smoking, left one for her kids: to stop a fall or wipe a nose or give a slap, depending. He'd been holding onto the picnic, the handles of two plastic bags double-looped around his wrist. Minding it and making a big deal out of minding it too, because the last time when Susan had been in charge she'd left the bag at the bus stop. A low throb in his wrist, he'd the handles wound that tight, and the farty smell of egg sandwiches along with the fumes of the bus making him feel a bit sick.

In the memory he doesn't see Susan, and this bothers him now as it bothered him then. That was the thing about his big sister: it was a relief when she wasn't with them, riling Ma up and agitating the atmosphere with her general carry-on. Yet when she wasn't there, he always felt the lack of her. She was being punished, most likely, left behind with one of the tougher aunties or locked into the box room for the day. Punished by exclusion. Because as Ma would often say, 'Slapping Susan was a complete waste of time.' Not that it ever stopped her.

And that's it – the memory. No beginning, no end, meaning little or nothing. Yet it still manages to catch him by the throat.

Frank leans forward, 'Actually, that was Ballyfermot I wanted, not Ballymun,' he says.

'Yeah, I know,' the taxi man grunts.

The first Dublin accent he's heard, apart from his own, in nearly twenty years – and that's about all he's getting of it.

*

The road sign for Ballyfermot gives him a start, like spotting the name of someone he once knew well in a newspaper headline. A few minutes later they are passing through the suburb of Palmerstown and Frank is struck by the overall beigeness: houses, walls, people, their faces.

At Cherry Orchard Hospital, the traffic tapers to a crawl. The hospital to the right, solid and bleak as ever and, still firmly in place, the laundry chimney that had been his view and constant companion during his three months there when he was a kid. He can feel Da now. Trying to get inside his head, shoulder up against it, pushing.

They draw up alongside the hospital gate, walls curving into the entrance, and it comes back to Frank, the lurch of the ambulance that night, the pause and stutter of the siren as if it had forgotten the words to its song. And him coming out of his delirium just long enough to see snowflakes turning against the black glass of the ambulance window and wondering how come he was sweating so much when outside it was cold enough for snow. He had asked where they were, and when the ambulance man said Cherry Orchard he'd thought it the loveliest name he'd ever heard.

The taxi man tuts at the traffic then switches on the radio. A voice comes out talking about money. Another voice over a phone line, shaking with nerves or possibly rage. The taxi man reaches out and switches the silence back on.

Frank remembers now the sound of the ambulance doors whacking back and the sensation of being hoisted up and lifted into the darkness and the cooling air. And looking up into the muddle of snow, he had got it into his head it was cherry blossom falling down on him.

He must have been ranting about it all during the illness anyhow, because after he got better Da bought him a book of the Chekov play. He was a fourteen-year-old youngfella who fancied himself as a bit of a brain, mainly because that's what everyone kept telling him. Yet he couldn't get beyond the first few pages of, what seemed to him, a boring old story about moany-arsed people with oddly spelt names. He'd kept turning back to Da's inscription – *To Francis, my namesake, who, unlike the author, got out alive. With fondness, Frank Senior* – and trying to understand at the time what the hell did it mean or why – why would his da write to him like that? Like he was a grown up, like they were strangers?

The taxi begins to move again; the cars break away from each other and Ballyfermot comes into view. Frank looks out the window. As far as he can see, nothing much has changed, apart from one modern-looking lump of a building further down the road. It looks like the same old, bland old Ballyer that it always was. Rows of concrete-grey shops under a dirty-dishcloth sky. Even the weather is utterly familiar: stagnant and damp. The threat of rain that might or might not bother to fall.

He can't remember the address. Not the name of the road, not even the number of the door – it just seems to have fallen out of his head.

He can remember everything else though: that the road is long and formed into a loop, and that the house is on the far end of the loop, and that the turn for the road is coming up soon. He begins to feel queasy; in his gut, the Aer Lingus breakfast shifts. And he wonders again, as he wondered while eating it, what had possessed him to order it because it certainly hadn't been hunger. Nostalgia then? For what? Sunday mornings, bunched up together in the little kitchen, steam running down the walls? Or Saturday nights when Ma and Da would come rolling home from the pub? Ma slapping rashers onto the pan. Da voicing the opinions he hadn't had the nerve to express in the pub, hammering them out on the Formica table. Ma agreeing with each revision, laughing at just the right moment. The waft crawling upstairs into Frank's half-sleep: black pudding, burnt rashers. Shite talk.

He presses his fingertips into his forehead, rotating the loose flesh against the bone of his skull. The skin on his face feels greasy and thick for the want of a shave, and even though his nose is stuffed from the flight, he can tell he doesn't smell the sweetest. He should really go to the house first, clean himself up a bit. A quick shave, a change

of shirt. But he isn't ready for the family, the neighbours
– all that.

'What time is it there?' Frank asks the driver, whose
finger even manages to look sardonic when it points to
the clock on the dashboard. Frank looks down at his own
watch, sees that it agrees.

Three minutes to eleven. All he has to do is say, 'If you
wouldn't mind taking the next right – just up along here.'

He holds the sentence in his head for a moment. But
the car skims past the turn and the moment has gone.

The taxi man speaks, startling Frank with the sudden rasp
of his voice.

'Where to?'

'Oh. Let's see, you know the church just up the road
there? If you could just –'

'Right.'

'Actually, maybe if you could, you know, pull in around
the corner down the road a bit and –'

'Right.'

'Or –'

He sees the eyebrows go up in the rear-view mirror.

'No, that'll be fine. Down that road there, near the
school, grand, that's grand.'

The car takes the broad corner, passing the slate-grey
church. Frank looks down at his feet.

The shock of the taxi fare: he feels like saying, Christ you
could travel from one end of India to the other for that.
He hands over a note and says nothing. The taxi man picks
up a pouch and begins pecking at coins. He opens it wider

and peers down into it. 'You home for good or a holiday?' he mutters as if he's talking to some little creature in the bottom of it.

'A fortnight,' Franks says, holding out his hand for the change.

'Listen – I do the the airport run, so when you're headin' back give us a shout – right? I'm only down the road. And I'll do you a good deal,' he pokes a business card at Frank, 'off the meter, like.'

'Oh, thanks,' Frank says, 'that's good of you.'

The taxi man shrugs. 'Yeah, well, business is crap is all.'

Frank slips the card into his pocket.

He pushes the haversack back into the seat, opens the front zip and edges his hand in. The haversack is bloated, the space tight. He can feel the taxi man watch as he rummages around. He pulls out a black tie, bit by bit, holding it up for a moment like a dead eel between his fingers. Through the mirror their eyes meet. The taxi man nods. Frank nods back.

On the kerbside he goes to work on his tie, slipping it under his collar, sliding the ends into place, planning the next little tie-making step in his head. He considers his entourage: one large suitcase bandaged in plastic – courtesy of Mumbai Airport security – and one bulky brown haversack plonked down beside it. His most recent mistakes scurry like mice through his head. Why hadn't he replied to Miriam's email, told her he had decided to come? Grand, if he couldn't face the house – but why hadn't he at least had a shave in the airport? Or at the very least, why hadn't he thought to get out of the taxi at one of the pubs down the road – had a wash, a quick drink to steady the nerves, maybe even asked the barman to hold on to the luggage for a while? Why? Why? *Why?*

Frank stops. From the school across the road comes the flat chant of children's voices. Choir practice. A phrase is repeated three, then four times. In between, a woman's voice calls out, 'Again. *And* again. Now and *gooood.*' He imagines her lifting her hands, holding the blend of voices and notes on her palms for one perfect second before letting them slip through her fingers. Frank thinks of his first job in India when, as a young teacher, he was railroaded into taking choir practice even though he hadn't a note in his head. His hands shaking as he tried to remember the hurried instructions the headmaster had given him. Dozens of keen brown eyes following his every move. Until suddenly he'd just got the hang of it. The pleasure then, in the power of his least little gesture. The music passing back and forth between himself and the children. Waves of sound on a small ocean. Every child bursting to please. One boy, an awkward child, had frightened him with the intensity of his emotion. His name gone now, but the face still there. The boy had his arm in a sling – he was a child who always had something bruised or broken.

Frank stands listening to the end of the song. His mind begins to quieten. He completes the knot in his tie, patting it into place.

A few minutes later he is struggling through the doors of the church, suitcase before him, big brown haversack like a chimpanzee up on his back. Frank keeps the boy in the choir in his head – the gapped front teeth, the flap-away

21

ears, the sling on his broken arm stiff with dirt. He pushes the luggage into a back corner under the balcony floor and then steps into a nearby pew. Dilip – that was the name of the child. One day he just stopped coming to school – vanished. Nobody seemed to know where or why.

The interior of the church settles around him. There's a chill, musty odour on the air: old incense and decades of sweat. The top half of the benches are filled with people. The last quarter empty. The bit in between sparsely populated. He glances up towards the altar – the coffin catches his eye. Too small. It seems way too small for Da. Da had been a big bloke, tall, with plenty of meat to go with it. Unless he had shrunk.

Frank sits down and begins sidling along the empty pew, moving in fits and starts, as if making room for non-existent people behind him. He takes Miriam's email from his pocket and reads it again.

Frankie, I'm sorry to tell you Da passed away yesterday – a sudden death. He was gone before he hit the ground so at least there was no suffering. I hope this message gets to you, Frankie. I got the address through the embassy who got it from the old school where you used to work. It's the only way I have of contacting you. Anyhow I'll hope for the best. Frankie, Ma is not well at all and it would mean a lot to her if you were here. She's an old woman now and what happened, well, it was a long time ago, Frankie. Anyway, I'll leave it there. It's been such a time. I really hope you can make it. But try to let me know, Miriam xxx.

Frank folds the email back into his pocket and moves up another space. Maybe all men feel this way in the end, he decides, that the coffin built for their father is built for a lesser man.

Beneath his line of vision he can make out the front-row mourners, banked together, solid and dark. Yet he can't bring himself to look directly at them, knowing full well that if he does he won't be able to stop himself from guessing who owns which head on whose shoulders; these people he would have grown up with, these now strangers.

He can't find anywhere to put his hands. He tries clasping them in front, then shoving them into the fold of his arms, then down into his jacket pockets. Finally, he grips them onto the bar of the pew in front.

The priest's voice drifts into the echo. 'If I speak in the tongues of men and of angels ...' And suddenly he thinks he sees Susan. He gets it into his head that she's over there, on the far side of the church, and that if he were to turn and look he would find her: hair tied back in a long black ponytail, dark-green coat on her straight Irish-dancer's back. He feels a bit shaken – disabled, almost. As if his legs don't belong to him. His stomach is bouncing. The breakfast churns. Air. He needs air.

*

Outside in the grey light, he loses his bearings – morning or evening? But if it were evening, it would have to be dark by now.

In the middle of the churchyard, the hearse is waiting, big square jaw open at the back, ready to suck the coffin in. A long Mercedes car for mourners is parked a little way behind it. Two funeral attendants stand nearby, heads close together, under-breath laughter and a night-before story. They see him and break apart, soft sprung steps taking them off in opposite directions. They remind him of FBI agents: the height, the long black coats, the haircuts, the inscrutable faces. And the broad shoulders of course: coffin-ledges. The Mercedes has three rows of seats and Frank wonders why they should need so many. It comes to him, then, the whole shape of the family will have changed by now: a husband, a wife maybe; sons, daughters, nieces, nephews. Grandchildren.

It begins to rain, sharp little pins on the skin: not heavy but spiteful – he'd forgotten Irish rain could be like that. One of the attendants opens the boot of the car and begins teasing out large black umbrellas. The bell tolls, a slow funeral toll. Frank presses the collar of his jacket into his neck and moves around to the side of the church, staying close to the churchyard's boundary wall. He notices long marks scrolled on the concrete – piss stains or rain stains, he can't decide which.

In a few minutes' time Da will be carried out, and he wonders whose shoulders will bear him: Johnny, the uncles, the cousins? Maybe they'll leave it up to the funeral attendants. Not that it really matters who takes him out, who sinks him into the clay. In a short time he'll be gone anyway. Worm-meat, as Advi once said.

Out of sight now, Frank steps into the alcove of the porch on this side of the church. A favourite spot when he was a kid: the door always locked – a place to see without being seen, to smoke and slag anyone who passed through the gate. He misses the smokes now, the company of them, the distraction they would bring.

He needs to think. But his mind is already blocked up with too many thoughts: his first monsoon in Bombay; Advi's father's funeral; the girl in the church with the dark-green coat; Da's coffin; the worms wiggling in the ground in a knot of greedy anticipation. The green coat again.

He comes back to his first monsoon.

Up on the flat roof with Advi and Gopal. Stoned, of course, which had lit up the details and made everything seem oh so profound. Advi's father not long dead. Frank not that long in India. The sky, one minute a hearth of orange and red, the next splitting like the skin on an over-ripe fruit. In a matter of moments, people on the streets below were wading through water, schoolbags and briefcases over their heads. It was high tide and across the rooftops they could see the Gateway of India being bashed by sea waves. It had looked like a ship out at sea. Youngfellas making a run at the waves, spindly legs and arms frantically waggling. After a while all visibility was lost to a thick dirty curtain of rain. They'd squeezed under the shelter, a sort of makeshift construction on the east side of the roof, Frank rolling another joint, the other two telling funeral stories. At first he hadn't been sure if they were having him on – Advi with his vultures, Gopal with his burning widows, although by then, even just a few short weeks into his first year, nothing would have surprised him about India. Advi told them that when his father died he was laid out on a slab at the top of a tower, under an open sky. Vultures looping overhead. The Tower of Silence, this place was called. The name alone had chimed in Frank's head. 'You mean you don't put him in a coffin?'

'Oh, no, no. Just lay him out naked.'

'Not a shroud or a blanket or something?'

'Nope. Total birthday suit, man. Go out as you've come in.'

'And the vultures actually, you know, actually –?'

'Eat him?' Advi said. 'They pick the bones clean – yum, they love it. It's the Parsi way.'

The idea had horrified Frank and he said so.

'Oh, come now, really – what difference does it make?' Advi asked. 'Coffin or not? Above the horizon or below? Worm-meat or vulture-feed? We're all fucked by then anyhow.'

It was the funniest thing they'd ever heard – or at least the dope had made it seem so. The three of them fell on the ground laughing. Advi and Gopal had rolled out from under the shelter. Frank had very nearly pissed himself, could hardly move or even see. Except for the odd glimpse through the beating rain – of a coffee-coloured face, a crescent of gleaming teeth, clothes plastered on two slender bodies, a hand reaching out to touch a blue-black head of glistening hair. And, of course, the first brief crossing of his mind that there may have been something more than friendship between his two new Indian friends.

*

Frank sees a man walking towards him, coming around from the front of the church, huddled into himself, smoking a cigarette. He can feel the man watching him.

The step slows and now he's standing right in front of him, uttering a cautious 'Frank?'

A small bloke, legs like two sticks in denim; could be any age from forty to sixty.

'Frankie, is that you? Jaysus, it is.' The man smiles, showing a bar of brown teeth. 'Ah, it's great to see you it is, great you could come, man, you look bleedin' great you do, like a – I don't know – banker or a politician or some big bleedin' shot anyway. How've you been, where've you been even? Like, everyone thought you were – you know – *dead*. Or somethin'.'

The man's handshake is weak, his voice has a womanish whine to it. Frank tries to find a place for him in his memory. A neighbour? A friend of Johnny's? A relative then? Whoever he is, he stinks of last night's beer.

'Sorry to hear about the Da, Frankie, and that. I know, now, we had our differences but, like, he wasn't the worst.'

'Thanks,' Frank says.

'I wouldn't mind but I only seen him the other day. Ah yeah. We passed each other on the road, like. I didn't speak to him or nothin' but he looked great, he did, Frankie.'

Over the man's shoulder Frank sees the churchyard filling: legs, elbows, a bloom of black umbrellas. There's a smell of cigarettes, little hums of reverent chatter. He is struck by how big everything is: the cars, the people – especially the people.

The man squints up at the rain then edges in under the lip of the roof. He starts talking again. 'Here, Miriam was only sayin' about you last night at the removal and that the way she didn't know what to do about finding you and all and she'd sent a whatyoucallit email and was –'

'I've only just arrived, haven't had a chance yet to – how is she anyway?'

'Well, like, I wasn't actually talkin' to her meself, I sort of more overheard her, like. She was a bit upset about poor old Susan and that. Brings it all back doesn't it – a funeral?'

'Yes, yes, it does.'

'Ah, she was a lovely girl, Susan. A bit wild, but sure so fuckin' wha'? Here, where is it you are now in anyway – Australia or somewhere is it?'

'India.'

'India! Jaysus, what the fuck were you doin' there? India! Ah, don't tell me, Frank – smoker's paradise, eh? I mighta bleedin' known. Ghanji on the Ganges and all that – wha'?'

'Ah, I gave that up a long time ago. I live there now.'

'Oh. And what do you do there – like, how do you spend your time?'

'I work.'

'Oh right, yeah.'

'I'm in education.'

'Ah, you always had it up there, Frankie.' He tips the side of his head. 'So what are you, like, a teacher and that?'

'I used to be a teacher. It's more administration now. For a charity.'

'What, like, you work for nothin'?'

'No. It's – it's difficult to explain.'

'Oh.' The man looks away – disappointed or embarrassed, Frank can't tell which.

He can't find the hearse – the crowd, the brollies have blotted it out. He's beginning to think he's missed Da's exit when the murmuring voices suddenly stop and, although he can't see the church door from here, he can tell the coffin is coming out. The crowd parts. A space is made around the hearse and at last he sees the high-gloss finish of coffin wood. There's a funeral attendant at each side: shoulders of experience keeping everything steady. The rest of the pall-bearers are of uneven height. Something familiar about one man, the shape of the profile, the dip of the head. The coffin is hoisted then lowered towards the opened back of the hearse. It still looks too small.

The funeral attendants stand aside and he can see now that the man who had looked familiar is Johnny. He watches his brother pass through the crowd to the far side of the churchyard, joining two men by the railings. He looks old; older than he should do anyhow. Hands in the trouser pockets of a suit that is way too big for him. He doesn't seem to notice the rain. He reminds Frank of a chicken, the way he stands, half talking to his mates, half looking around with an agitated eye.

'For how long were you there in anyway, Frankie?' the man says then.

'In India? About twelve years.'

'I thought you went, you know, after Susan?'

'Well, yeah, I went to London first, then India.'

'And you never went back to the old house after – you don't mind me askin'?'

'No, and no I didn't.'

'Ah, they done it up lovely after, Frankie. Brand new. Not a mark on it. Your ma does keep it like a little palace, she does. Ah, look – there's Miriam now. Looks great, doesn't she, Frankie?'

He sees her then, a middle-aged woman, well preserved, well dressed. A tall man beside her, obviously the husband, two tall sons who are almost men.

'She done well for herself. Married a solicitor, she did. That's him. Kids go to college and all. Are you married yourself, Frankie?

'No.'

'Kids?'

'No.'

'Not that you know of in anyway – wha'?' The man nudges the air and gives a little laugh.

'No,' Frank says. 'I've none.'

The man lights another cigarette then takes a step closer to Frank. There's something needy in the gesture, like he's desperate to hold on to his company. Frank looks away. He sees Ma now. He sees her standing close to the hearse, surrounded by aunties who are buckled and harmless with age. Miriam's husband is holding an umbrella high over her head.

Ma's face. Her face, when he sees it. Not as old as he'd expected but just as hard. A man comes up to pay his respects; she rests a hand on his arm. Her slapping hand. He can't look at her face any more, only the hand. He thinks of it, now, as a separate entity, cleaning and polishing windows, doors, brasses, removing stains only she can see. He thinks of the sound of it slapping a leg, a face or folding into a fist to punch the back of a head. He thinks of it half drunk and slightly off kilter, flipping rashers onto the pan and later, floppy on the edge of the sofa, trying to smoke a cigarette. He thinks of it turning the key in the lock of the boxroom door, a voice above it. 'And you can fuckinwell STAY there.'

'Susan wasn't wild,' Frank says.

'No?'

'She was different.'

'Oh yeah, well of course, of course, I didn't mean like –'

Frank listens to the man beside him sucking on his cigarette, hawing it out in sharp, short breaths. After a minute he turns back to him. 'Were you thinking of going up to the graveyard yourself?'

'Ah, you know me, Frankie, I wouldn't like to intrude and that. I'll probably just go to the fuckin' pub after. Pay me respects then, you know?'

Frank looks at his thin face, cold sores around his lips, skin on his hand mauvish and blotched, his lip struggling with the tip of the cigarette. 'Look, could I ask you to do me a favour?' he says.

'Sure, man, of course you can. Just name it.'

Frank reaches into his pocket and pulls out a fifty euro note. He holds it towards the man. 'Could you keep it to yourself that, well, you know, you saw me here.'

'Ah, you don't have to give me that, Frank, honest you don't.'

He can see the man's hand is trembling to take the note. Frank presses it into his fingers. 'No, go on, really. Take it. Have a drink on me – I want you to. Just don't say anything about seeing me.'

'Sure, Frankie, if that's what you really want?'

'It's just … I mean, I just –'

'All right, Frankie, yeah, I know. I know. All right.'

The man scratches his face, then his hair. 'You haven't a fuckin' clue who I am, have you?'

'I'm sorry,' Frank says.

He shrugs and lifts his hand as if to shake Frank's, then seems to change his mind and settles on a half-salute. Frank watches him go, head down, shoulders hunched, close to the churchyard wall.

He looks over the churchyard: the arrangement of people, each to his own little group. The funeral attendants look like FBI agents again, sending out silent instructions. Everything shifts, everyone moves. There's a sound of car doors slamming, the spark-up of individual engines. A black-haired girl in a green coat hurries across the churchyard, dashes the butt of a cigarette to the ground and hops into the back of a car. The green coat he saw from the corner of his eye in the church. Not really like Susan, after all. Nothing like her, in fact.

The hearse budges towards the gate now, the coffin inside it snug between glass and chrome: a perfect fit. The long Mercedes, filled with shadows, following behind. They pass out onto the road, skim the far side of the railings, then disappear.

He imagines the hearse, the cortège behind it, skirting the roundabout, gliding past the school, the shops, the pub on the corner, before taking the turn into the road where Da lived all the days of his married life. He pictures it then, nosing along the slow, endless curve past the squeeze of houses he'd counted every day on his way home from school and the railings he'd sat on and the gates he'd swung out of and all the kerbs he'd battered with footballs and later then, much later, the hundreds of windows behind their veils of net that had followed him like eyes behind burkhas during the black weeks and days after Susan.

He takes the taxi man's card out of his pocket and waits for the churchyard to drain – of cars, of sound. Of people.

La Straniera

For L.J.

Ours was a large bedroom. Formerly two rooms knocked into one, it took up the entire top floor of a house we couldn't afford to live in.

Four long windows overlooked the gardens: two to the back, two facing front. At the far end of the room was a fireplace bunged up with dried flowers, over which hung a rust-mottled mirror. On winter nights the sash windows rattled us to sleep. In summer, with the back windows up, we could hear Mr Andrews' birds beeping and squeaking like squeezed soft toys in their aviary. The three beds were doubles and, like the house, had been inherited from distant relatives of my father. Babies had been made and born in our beds, people had slept and died in them, but I seemed to be the only one who lay awake at night and worried about such things. We had two wardrobes: a great big musty clump of mahogany shared by myself and Dora and another slimline, modern model that Tess had saved up for herself as soon as she started working. My mother, who had a bad leg, couldn't manage the stairs without considerable pain and so the bedroom became our own private world. On the rare occasion when my father stuck his nose round the door, he always made a remark about how you could park a bus in it. For all that, it never seemed big enough for Lucia.

Before she arrived we knew only this about her – she was our cousin, in her mid-twenties or maybe a little older. She'd been born and raised on the continent; her father was my mother's eldest brother; her mother was from the west or somewhere.

We were told she was one of us, but the very word 'Lucia' seemed distant and odd and felt more like a jelly sweet than a name in my mouth.

Our room gleamed for her arrival. My father's two sisters, Brenda and Margaret, collected her from the train station and brought her to our house, where, along with my mother, they puffed and panted up the three flights of stairs to help her unpack. They swooned over the beautiful clothes that came slithering out of her luggage, bleated over her accent, her perfume, her dancer's posture, asked umpteen questions about her mother, her father and continental living. Then they all went back down the stairs and left us alone to deal with each other.

The mantel shelf quickly filled up with her bits: combs, brushes, foreign cosmetics. Her clothes bullied ours to the back of both wardrobes. There were coats and dresses lolling on the end of her bed, twirls of dirty underwear on the floor; hats and scarves heaped on the old kitchen table that Dad and Mr Andrews (who'd nearly had a heart attack in the process) had hosted up the stairs so Dora and I would have somewhere to do our homework and Tess could study the French she was taking at night school.

Lucia was clotty. She could be rude in her comments, ungrateful in her manner and inconsiderate in the extreme – locking herself in the bathroom for an age while the rest of us had to make do with the stinky outdoor toilet with the wind hooshing under its door. From the first, it was clear she was going to be a disruption. But for all that, she shone her own peculiar light on the small routines of our lives. She dressed us in her clothes and jewellery, sprayed us with perfume and lacquer. She taught us bits of foreign languages: songs in German and French, Italian love-words and curses. She showed Dora how to do ballet pliés and how to dance sideways like an Egyptian. She drew our names in fancy letterings and gave Tess a beauty lesson in how to make her eyelashes black. She thrilled us to the bone with her Greta Garbo accent telling stories of cocktails and cities and men.

My father sometimes talked to her about politics 'over there', or he might ask questions about the various people who called on her father, all of whom, he seemed to presume, were 'interesting'.

Mother took great care of her, giving her the best bits of meat, which she seldom ate, and ironing her clothes, which would end up being thrown in a ball on the floor. 'And how are you feeling now?' she would often ask, as if moments ago Lucia had been poorly. Occasionally she called her into the parlour for 'a quick word in private'.

Lucia was nearest in age to Tess, but they never really hit it off. Nor did she have a whole lot of time for me, which I presumed had something to do with my illness – for the previous three months everything seemed to have something to do with my illness. She was really at her best with Dora who, at ten years old, was our youngest. She took her on afternoon outings and I was sometimes allowed to tag along if Mother felt I was 'up to it'. Even after two months of convalescence I was still thought to be a bit dawny-looking and in need of watching. But I didn't feel dawny at all – I felt strong, if only they'd let me be strong. I felt I could skip across all the acres of sand on Sandymount beach, climb up and walk along every wall on the way there, swim for miles through the sea all the way out to Howth. And I had such an appetite. I wanted to eat all around me, every sandwich on the plate, every spud in the stew pot. In the grocer's I wanted to pick up the whole wheel of cheese and gnaw my way through it. Hungry and strong – that's how I felt inside. And I could never understand why, after a few running strides in the fresh air, my breath grew short and seemed to be trying to get back inside my lungs, or why, after a few morsels of food, my stomach felt full and my tongue grew dead in my mouth.

Lucia brought Dora and me to places we'd only ever seen from the outside: high-ceilinged banks where she changed foreign money; picture houses where she often left us alone for an hour or more. She left us again outside a basement flat on Harcourt Street and, when she came out, swore us to secrecy then bought us cream buns for tea. On these outings strangers sometimes spoke to her – usually men. And once in Bewley's she pretended to one of them that we were foreign too, and as he spoke to us, slow word by slow word, we nearly choked into our napkins trying to stop ourselves from laughing. Another time in Stephen's Green a man, older than my father, although much more handsome, asked her out to dinner.

*

Lucia turned her face in the mirror: full profile, three-quarters profile, hat on, hat off. She asked us again about the cast in her eye – was it more noticeable like this or like that? Did we think it spoiled her looks? Her chances of catching a husband then? It became a habit, this turning about in the mirror and asking about her eye.

And I thought it odd, and even a bit mean of her, to go on and on about it when both my sisters had a similar affliction – a family weakness, which, up till then, we had all more or less pretended not to notice.

'I just wish Lucia didn't speak her mind quite so much,' I heard Mother say to my father one evening after Lucia had told my aunt Brenda that her new green coat made her look like a monument, and then, when Tess's fiancé, Pat, was describing his job, she interrupted him to ask if it didn't make him want to weep with boredom.

'I just wish Lucia gave a little more of herself,' Mother added a little while later, referring to Lucia's third refusal in a row to go out to tea with Aunt Margaret.

My father rattled his newspaper. 'More of herself! More! Jesus, do you not think now we might have enough?'

*

One night I woke and saw Lucia at the far end of the room looking into the fireplace mirror. It was the night before Tess went on her cycling holiday. Dora – who wouldn't wake up if the house were bombed from under her – was sleeping beside me and I was grateful to see Tess across the room, already awake and half out of bed.

'What are you doing?' Tess asked her.

'Looking at them.'

Tess switched on the lamp, and a yellow web spread over the middle of the room. Behind it, a back view of Lucia, long and thin in her nightdress, her face a dim, watery mask in the mirror.

'Who? Lucia, who?' Tess asked.

Lucia said a few foreign words, stopped then continued in English, 'I know they are in there. I almost see them. But when I look, they are gone. And in a moment, I almost see them again.'

'For God's sake, Lucia!' Tess said, flipping back the bedclothes and padding up the room. 'I'm supposed to be going on holiday tomorrow – in case you give a damn.'

I shut my eyes tight and snuggled back down into Dora's safe warmth. Tess got Lucia back into bed and the night lamp went out and soon I could hear Tess's deep breathing. I knew Lucia was lying there with her eyes wide open and could hear the shivery sound of her whispers like someone praying in the dark.

I thought of the marble tiles on the wall of our bathroom and how, whenever I happened to be sitting on the toilet, I could see – or almost see – groups of things in them and how I never seemed to see the same group twice. I tried to remember the last lot: angels' heads growing out of a stalk.

A man with a flat cap. A woman with no eyes and hair like a mermaid. A pig's head like you'd see in the butcher's window.

*

Tess came back from her cycling holiday, took one look at the state of our bedroom and announced she was going to stay with the aunties. And we missed her so much, Dora and I, because, even though she still popped in for a visit, she mostly talked to Mother in the kitchen about the plans for her wedding and refused to come up to our room. We were all so proud of Tess: she worked behind a counter in the Brown Thomas shop and you couldn't get much swankier than that, as my father liked to say. Sometimes when we went into town we would stand at the window pretending to look at the display inside and spy on her. It was something to show our friends from school. She might be serving a customer or chatting to a colleague or polishing the glass on her counter: our big sister, with her slim hips and her high heels and her smart hairstyle and her long, elegant hands with the twinkle of an engagement ring when she turned it under the light.

'The poshest shop in the whole city,' I heard Dora say to Lucia on the bus into town. 'Oh, wait till you see her!'

'I've already seen her,' Lucia mumbled without turning her head from the window.

'No, no, I mean in the shop. In it. I know you've already seen her and the shop too, but, but – see, she's back from her holiday now and you haven't, you didn't …' Dora broke off, unable to find the sense she'd been seeking. I could tell she was already worried that Tess behind the counter of the

41

Brown Thomas shop would prove to be a disappointment to Lucia. I was seated behind them, and for the whole journey Lucia, her face on the glass of the window, the curve of fur at her throat, her hat drawn down over one eye, didn't budge an inch. For the first time I began to dislike my cousin.

Dora kept talking to her, asking questions that remained unanswered, fidgeting excitedly on her seat, the bobble of her hat wobbling on the top of her little head; giving, giving, giving. And all Lucia could return for the entire journey was a half-uttered, 'I've already seen her.'

I thought her false and spoilt then, and utterly selfish. I resented her everything: her foreign voice and her film-star clothes and the way she always had to make heads turn whenever we walked into a café. The way she quizzed waiters as if they were her inferiors then ordered food she hardly ate. The way she threw her money around but never brought so much as a bar of chocolate home for Mother. The way she bribed us to tell lies. But most of all for the way she had made Tess seem ordinary, had taken the adventure out of her cycling holiday, the romance out of her French lessons and the glamour off the man she would marry.

We came up near College Green and Dora stood up, placed one knee on the seat and, leaning into Lucia, whispered, 'She won't be anywhere near as beautiful as you.'

And I felt like giving my little sister a slap. But instead I said, 'Sit down, Dora – you'll fall.'

*

I started to become afraid of my cousin soon after that and found myself checking through the crack in the door before entering a room to see if she was in it. Or if I came across her somewhere unexpectedly, say the parlour or out in the garden, muttering an excuse and scuttling away. Then she stopped sleeping and, because there was something unsettling about the thought of her being awake while I was asleep, I stopped sleeping too.

The only rest I had was when she went out for the evening: then I'd go up to bed early and immediately pass out. But as soon as the doorknob began to turn, my eyes would pop open. Sometimes she'd sit by the front window, smoking in the dark, looking out as if she were waiting for someone. Or maybe she'd stand staring into the mirror again. Mostly she'd just do what I was doing, which was lie on my back, wide-awake and silent, gazing up at my own little patch of the ceiling.

Dora went back to school. It had been decided that a couple more weeks' convalescence would do me no harm so I was kept home. Apart from Mother, who spent most of her time in the kitchen or pottering in the back garden, I was alone in the house with Lucia. I tried to stay with Mother, but she kept sending me off to keep Lucia company or telling the pair of us to go out and get some fresh air, and I had to keep pretending I didn't feel up to it, and the more I pretended the worse I felt, and the worse I felt the more dawny I looked and then the longer I was kept out of school.

In the mornings Mother would send me up with a tray: milky coffee, bread and jam, because that's all she would take for breakfast. If there was a letter from her father I'd bring that too. And I hated going up to our room on my own, never knowing which way she might be, the dread of her voice when I turned the last flight of stairs, singing to itself, as it had started to do. Sometimes, I would see her head under the covers, pretending to be asleep, the sprout of her black hair on top, the peculiar whiff of her medicine.

'What's she doing now?' Mother asked when I came back down.

'She's singing, Mother.'

'Well now, that's a good sign – she must be a bit happier in herself so.'

But there was nothing happy about Lucia's song or the way that she sang it.

*

In the kitchen we could hear her thundering over the long floor of our bedroom.

'Where's Her Highness?' Aunt Brenda asked, coming into the kitchen.

Mother lifted her hand and pointed twice to the ceiling.

'No sign of her going back then …?'

'No,' Mother said.

'They've a cheek all right,' Margaret said, following behind Brenda. 'I mean to say, have you not got enough to be doing?'

'He's asked me to keep her another while.'

'For God's sake, Anna – how much longer?' Brenda gasped. 'It's been over six weeks.'

'Well, he thinks it's good for her to be here and –'

'Good for her, maybe,' Brenda said.

'The way he sees it, she's been doing well, she has the girls for company and has even made a few friends. No disasters anyway, thank God.'

'Worse luck for you,' Margaret said, rooting in her handbag and pulling out her fags.

'What do you mean?'

'Well – are they going to leave her here forever, just because she's been behaving herself?'

I went up to the hall and sat on the chair outside Mother's bedroom door to reread the letter Tess had sent to me. It was written on Brown Thomas notepaper with a little, blurred drawing of the shopfront on the top that I felt didn't do it much justice. Tess said she was fed up with the aunties and their spinstery ways, but it was better than putting up with Lucia and her continental clottiness, not to mention the way she treated Pat – either playing up to him or else being downright insulting.

A noise distracted me from the top of the house and as I stood up something caught my eye. I looked through the stairwell and there was Lucia at the top banister. For a minute I thought she was talking to me and, because I couldn't hear, began to climb the stairs. On the second flight, I saw then she was looking up, not down – her face turned to the skylight. She was talking to the air, wittering to herself in a muddle of foreign and English words, as if she were a human wireless that someone was trying to tune.

'Yes, but where does she go when she goes out in the evenings?' Aunt Margaret was saying when I came back down to the kitchen.

'She eats out.'

'What do you mean eats out? *Where?*'

'With her friends.'

'What friends?'

'All I know is she stays upstairs most of the day and –'

'Doing what?' Brenda asked.

'Reading, drawing, sometimes dancing. Resting – he said she was to have plenty of rest. Then she comes down in the evening and goes out to meet her friends. And she looks fine and seems fine and comes home at a reasonable hour. And that's good enough for me.'

'But the friends – who are these friends?'

'I'm her aunt not her jailer. And she's a grown woman, Margaret.'

'*Exactly,*' Aunt Margaret said.

*

In my dream one of the birds had escaped from Mr Andrews' aviary and the rest of the birds were screaming at it to come back inside. I could see them bouncing off the wire cage, their brittle claws catching on the mesh, their little heads turned sideways. And then above all their angry racket another, sharper sound came – a peck on the windowpane. And in the dream I said, 'Oh no, the escaped bird, what am I supposed to do now? How am I supposed to get it away from our window and back into the aviary?' Another peck – harder this time – and I thought, Oh no it must be one of the bigger birds, and hoped not the cockatiel with its hooked, determined beak that I'd seen tear the hand off Mr Andrews one time.

My eyes opened. My heart was drumming, my nightie stuck to me with the sweat. I looked up at the window behind the bed, but there was only a glaze of black sky above the lace half-curtain. The peck came again; a few seconds' silence, then another one. I pulled myself up and looked into the room – Lucia's bed was empty.

I reached across Dora and lifted the hem of the curtain: a few small stones were sitting on the windowsill. Down in the garden, I saw on the ground near the outside toilet a bag, coat and one shoe. Then I saw Lucia. She was rummaging for stones from Mother's ornamental border. The birds had quietened down, just a random squawk or squeal, and I guessed she had got through the side gap of Mr Andrews' gate, crossed his garden then climbed over our high wall onto the roof of the toilet before dropping down. Lucia stood up and gave a little stagger, steadied herself and staggered again. To the east, the sky was starting to redden and a slit of dawn-light was trying to get through.

I imagined myself sneaking all the way down the stairs in the cold, dark air, turning for the kitchen stairs, then having to search for the big key to the back door before dragging a chair through the pantry, standing on it, unbolting and unlocking the door: all that before the ordeal of dragging Lucia through the sleeping house.

I glanced down at Dora, still snoring away. A stone whacked off the window and I jumped. When I looked down Lucia was looking straight up at me, her clothes torn, her hair out like a bush, a startled light in her eye.

Dora stirred in the bed and then woke. 'What? What is it?' she whispered.

'Lucia. I think she's drunk.'

'Drunk!'

I let the curtain drop and moved to get out of the bed. Then Dora grabbed my arm. 'Don't,' she said.

'But Dora?'

'Let her go round the front and ring the doorbell.'

'She'll waken Mother.'

'Let her.'

'But why, Dora? They'll send her home.'

'They'll send her home and I'll be glad because I don't like her any more,' Dora said.

I slid back down into the bed, and for a while Dora and I lay side by side holding hands. After a while the pecking stopped, or at least we fell asleep.

In the morning her bed was still empty.

I crossed the room and stared down into it, wondering what to do. The bed was unmade – as it usually was – and the letter that had arrived yesterday from her father was lying where she'd left it on the pillow. *Cara Mia* it began and finished with *Bacci di Babbo*. I picked up the letter and studied my uncle's Irish handwriting, the same spindled slant as my mother and Tess, and read all the foreign words that he'd written, as if I could find a meaning or a hint in them as to where Lucia might be.

It was Sunday morning, the house still quiet, and I tipped down through it, peeping into each room on the way and not a sign of Lucia.

In the kitchen, all of those things that had seemed so difficult last night came easily now: the big key on the dresser, the chair across the pantry floor, the bolts, the lock, opening the door, stepping outside.

Mother's small garden was warming to the day – the spangle of dew on the grass, flowers neat in their little beds according to shape and colour. And Lucia's coat, shoe and bag still on the ground. For a moment I hoped. But it was a small garden with no place to hide other than inside the toilet, and all I could see through its half-opened door was a lime-crusted toilet bowl and a long, rusty chain. With my foot, I brushed the scatter of pebbles from the path back into the flowerbeds.

When I came inside Dora was shouting, 'Lucia isn't here. Lucia didn't come home! Lucia! Lucia! Oh God, oh God, where's Lucia?'

*

Once the policeman appeared, we spilled all the beans – the man in Stephen's Green, the afternoon we waited outside the flat on Harcourt Street, the times she left us alone in the picture house. Dora could only remember those details that directly concerned Lucia – a joke she'd made or the fur coat she'd tried on, pretending to buy. I remembered everything else: the colour of the suit on the man in Stephens' Green, the number of the door on Harcourt Street. I knew how much money and time she had spent and where she had spent it. I told about her staying in bed all day, about her whispering to herself in the middle of the night and about shouting at the woman in the chemist who wouldn't give her what she wanted. I told everything and anything I could recall except for the one thing that I would never forget nor mention again, not even to Dora. And that was the sound of the stones pecking off the window and the birds from the aviary screaming in anger and the sight of Lucia gently swaying down in our back garden, one arm reaching up to me, the flat of her palm stretched out.

*

A day later, Lucia was found, although she never came back to our house. My father took the day off work and there were the voices of strangers in our parlour: policemen, a detective, a doctor in a pinstriped suit.

That evening her luggage was pulled down from the attic and the aunties puffed and panted back up all the stairs to our bedroom. Mother washed and ironed her dirty laundry then insisted on carrying the stack up the stairs by herself. Tess removed the bric-a-brac from the mantelpiece shelf and wrapped each item in tissue. Brenda released all the clothes from the wardrobe and layered them across my bed. Aunt Margaret made a list. Then silently, slowly, the aunties and Mother folded each item back into itself and arranged them into the open cases.

Dora asked if Lucia was going home to her parents now and Mother shook her head. Then Dora started to cry and asked where was she going then if not home.

Brenda said, 'She'll be going somewhere they know how to take care of her.'

But she never told us who they were.

Saint Stephenses Day

On the first bus Norman fell off the seat. One minute he was kneeling up pretending to be the driver. The next he was flat out on his back, feet in the air, chubby face peering out between his two bare legs. The face all shocked although Billy couldn't see why – after all, Ma had warned him enough times, 'If you don't sit up properly you'll fall off that seat.'

They always went inside, past the conductor's spot under the stairs and then right down to the end, Billy and Norman on the long seat behind the driver, Ma on the small seat opposite with her back to the rest of the passengers. If it was a Sunday or a special day like today, the day after Christmas, then Da would be with them and he'd sit on the same seat as Ma.

The minute they got on the bus Norman had started. He pushed past Da and went barrelling off down the aisle on his own, shouting his head off, 'Look, Ma, look, there's no one in our place, there's no one in our place!'

Billy hated the way his little brother always had to call it 'our place', and he hated too how anytime they'd get on a bus, if the back seat was already taken he'd get in a huff and spend the whole journey staring at whoever it was that got there before them.

Once when they were all on the bus together Billy had decided to say so: 'It's not *our* place, Norman. We don't own it – do we? It belongs to everyone – isn't that right, Da? Doesn't it? Doesn't it belong to everyone?'

'That's right, Billy,' Da had said, 'everything belongs to everyone. We're all republicans now.'

Billy had been delighted that Da had agreed with him, even though he wasn't sure if the republican bit had been meant as some sort of a joke. Because it was hard to tell with Da sometimes. He had the sort of eyes that made him look as if he might burst out laughing any second. But at the same time, you wouldn't see him laughing all that much.

When Norman fell off the seat, he fell off backwards. They were on the way to visit Aunt Vera. Billy didn't mind visiting Vera any other day of the year, except for the day after Christmas. To have to leave the cosiness of his own house: the rug by the fire where he lay half watching telly, half reading his *Beano* annual, his hand slipping into the Selection Box here and there to tease another piece off a Curly Wurly bar when Ma's back was turned. To have to go all the way over to the far side of town, wait in the cold for the two buses that would take them there – and for what? A glass of lemonade and a finger of pudding that they could just as easily have had at home, seeing as how Ma had made it for Aunt Vera in the first place. He didn't want to have to sit on the big sofa that made his legs look extra skinny and his feet not able to touch the ground. And then be told to stop fidgeting every minute when it wasn't even his fault because the cover on the sofa was slippy.

Nor did he want to spend hours listening to Ma walking around the big posh house going, 'Oh, isn't that only lovely now?' or 'Is that new, Vera? God, it's gorgeous!'

Aunt Vera was all right – she was Ma's sister. She even looked like Ma, only more done up. They were nearly the same age, but because Aunt Vera got married years before Ma did, her kids were much older. Uncle Tod was all right too, even if he was a bit showy-off. He had a big red nose that made him look as if he always had a cold and he drove a big green car called a Rover like it was a dog and inside it, in the shelf on the back window, was a folded checked rug that Ma said was for going on picnics.

It was the grown-up cousins Billy wasn't that keen on. Always trying to be funny and jeering at his lisp in a round-about way, asking him questions with lispy answers like what was the proper name for the day after Christmas. Then showing off their old toys that you weren't allowed touch, like model airplanes and Lego sets with not even one piece missing. The eldest son was a trainee pilot. The youngest was a girl called Mairead. The two boys in the middle went to a school that had its own scarf called Castleknock College. One of them hardly ever came out of his room and Ma said that was because he was a bit odd. He had spots all over his face and little dents in the skin on the back of his neck that Norman wouldn't stop staring at. The other one practised golf into Tupperware cups out the back garden, and even in the sitting-room he'd stand swinging an invisible golf stick when he was watching the telly. Sometimes the pilot was there and sometimes he was away. But even when he was away, it still seemed like he was there because Aunt Vera couldn't stop talking about him, and there was this big framed photograph of his face over the mantelpiece and every time you looked up you could see him grinning sideways out from under his cap. Billy didn't like him most of all. When he was there, he'd pour out the lemonade and say, 'Ooo-K, kiddo – say when?' and then Norman would start shouting, 'When what? What when? I don't know what you mean by when!'

But the worst thing about the pilot was the minute they walked in the door he'd always have to go, 'Uh oh, watch out, danger about, here come the terrible twins!' even though he knew right well they couldn't be twins because Billy was nearly three years older than Norman, even if he wasn't all that much taller, and nowhere near as fat.

When Norman fell backwards off the seat, there was hardly anyone in the downstairs of the bus. Except for an old man with a noddy head sitting on the edge of his seat with one foot stuck out on the aisle. And a girl in a miniskirt sitting just inside the door. She was wearing a headscarf covered with paw-prints and she made Billy think of Ma's youngest sister, Maureen.

'Hey, Ma – will Maureen be coming today?' Billy asked, as they made their way down the aisle after Norman.

'Not today, love,' Ma said.

'Ah, Ma, why?'

'I don't know, she's not well or something.'

'But she didn't come last year either! Ma, why is she not coming again? That's not fair, Ma, it's just not fair!'

'Ah, what can I do about it, Billy?' Ma said. 'I can't drag her over by the scruff of the neck – can I?' Then she pushed him on past the old man, through a pong of porter and farts that was so disgusting it made him forget for a minute all about Maureen.

Billy liked his Aunty Maureen better than anyone because she was nice to look at and because she was funny as well. On the day after Christmas Day she always took the same bus home as them as far as town, even though Aunt Vera's husband would have already offered to drive her home. It was like she was saying she preferred to go with Ma and Da. It was like she was on their side.

On the bus she would make loads of remarks about Aunt Vera's family that Ma always pretended not to enjoy. She called Vera's husband Rudolph on account of his nose, and once she said that Mairead one was a right little granny that could do with a good toe up the ho, ho, ho. By then Norman would be fast asleep with his mouth hanging open and Billy would stay as quiet as he could so no one would notice him sitting with the adults listening to Maureen. The last time they were on the bus with Maureen was the best ever. She said it'd make you laugh, them and their notions, when they didn't even own the house and only lived there because it came as part of Rudolph's job and that they better watch it because as soon as he kicked the bucket they'd all be turfed out on their ear. And Ma had said, 'Oh, that's a terrible thing to say, Maureen.'

Then Maureen said she didn't care if it was or wasn't, it was all just for show anyhow: the posh house, the french doors and the big black piano, for feck sake, that nobody even knew how to play.

'Da knew how to play it!' Billy had said. 'And we don't even have a piano!'

'That's right, Billy, your Da showed them!' Maureen said and clapped her hands into the air. Then they all smiled for a minute at the memory of Da, the quiet way he had sat down at the piano and put his glass of whiskey on top of it, fixing the bit of lace beneath it so as not to leave a stain, and then his hands knowing exactly where to go – up and down the black and white keys until out came all these songs that everyone knew. 'Silent Night' and 'Moon River' and 'Rudolph the Red-Nosed Reindeer' that had made Norman and Billy laugh so much, thinking about Uncle Tod, that they'd had to hide behind the sofa.

Billy had missed Aunty Maureen last year. And now he was going to miss her again.

'I bet they won't even be in, Ma.'

'What are you talkin' about?'

'Aunt Vera and them, I bet they won't even be there.'

'Of course they'll be there.'

'Yeah? Well, they weren't in last year. Do you not remember we had to wait? In the rain and all, wait. And by the time –'

'That was a mix-up, Billy, and it won't happen again. So there's no need for you to go bringing it up now – do you hear me?'

Ma gave him one of her looks. Then she sat down in her usual place with her nose stuck up to the window.

Billy hung back for a moment. Norman had already hauled himself up onto the seat and now he was kneeling, his face an inch or so from the glass of what Da called the cockpit. The shadow of the driver locked inside. Billy watched his little brother shift his reflection to fit over the back of the driver's head, then, clutching onto the back of the seat, stiffen his arms straight out and sway with the bus from side to side. He revved and braked and beeped and ding-alinged until after a few seconds Norman had become, not only the driver, but also the bus.

'What's the matter with you now?' Ma asked Billy. 'Why don't you sit down?'

Billy shrugged. He didn't know what was the matter with him now, except that it had something to do with Norman. Nothing in the world would make him want do what Norman was doing acting like a baby. Yet in his heart he wished that he could just disappear the way Norman disappeared pretending to be the driver, pretending to be the bus.

'Where's Da?' he asked.

'Talking to the conductor,' Ma said. 'Now sit bloody down.'

When Norman fell backwards off the seat and cracked his head, Billy was sitting well away from him, even though Ma had given him the nod to move right up beside his little brother, in case he should fall. She gave him the nod and then just forgot all about it because she was too busy looking out the window. Billy didn't want to sit beside Norman anyway, not till the bus had got clear away from their estate and the chance of anyone from school getting on was gone by. Already Billy was too warm, the heat from the engine breathing up his legs. But he kept his coat on because he knew that any minute now Norman would want to take his one off, and then they'd both be there on the long back seat, looking like saps, all dressed up in their matching clothes that Ma called 'rig-outs'.

57

Ma had knit the jumpers herself; for weeks she'd been at it, vicious needles snapping at each other while she watched the telly, and a string of wool slowly making its way up to her from a basket at her feet like she was some sort of a snake-charmer.

'Who's that one for?' Billy had asked.

'Norman, I think,' Ma had said, lifting it up and guessing the measurement.

'What colour will my one be?' Billy had asked then, even though he knew by the knot in his stomach what her answer would be.

'Wine. The same as this. Both wine.'

'Ah, Ma, can I not have me own colour? At least something that's different to Norman's.'

'The wool is bought. Anyway, wine is a lovely winter colour. So I don't want to hear another whine out of you.'

'Whine or wine?' Norman had asked, and Ma had laughed and plucked his fat cheek, because she always laughed at Norman's stupid jokes.

The bus was jigging past the big church at Killester. Da was still down near the platform talking to the conductor.

'Can I sit beside you, Ma?' Billy askèd. 'It's too hot here.'

'No, your Da is sitting there,' Ma said, patting the place she had saved for Da, and Billy thought there was something greedy about the way she was always trying to keep Da all to herself.

'Can I not sit there for just a minute, Ma?'

'He'll be down now, Billy,' Ma said. 'Stop it, will you, like a good boy, please?'

Then she looked out the window again. Billy looked out the same window and tried to see through her eyes: the houses rattling past, the bony winter trees and the shops all closed for the day after Christmas Day. At least this year you could see out the window. Last year there had been rain so the glass was foggy and Billy had got told off for asking where they were every five minutes. Then he got told off some more for nagging about being late for Aunt Vera's. Ma had said that he was far too much of a worrier and that Aunt Vera's house would still be standing when they got there. Ma had been right: the house was still there, but there had been nobody in it. And because Da had said there was no point in wasting a journey, they had waited.

It had been all right for a while: the porch where they sheltered out of the rain like a little room with a brick half-wall on each side and a horseshoe-shaped arch that you went through to get to the front door. There were fairy lights like stars on the curve of the arch over their heads and at least it was dry in there, as Ma had said about ten times. Now and then Da had looked at his watch and said, 'We'll give them a few more minutes.' They had played I Spy. But after a while it was too dark to see and all the tall trees turned into shadows.

Then at last Da had said, 'Ah here, come on, enough is enough, we'll go –' And the minute he said that the lights from the car had burst into the drive and blasted right into their faces.

When Norman fell backwards off the seat and cracked the back of his head like an egg, the conductor was telling Da a big long story about something that happened in the pub the night before. He could hardly get the words out he was so busy laughing at his own story.

The conductor lived round the corner, and even though he had a son that was older than Billy he still looked much younger than Da. He looked like Cliff Richard, only with red eyes. The thought came to Billy then that Da looked like an old man. Not as old as the smelly man with the noddy head, but much, much older than any of the other Das on the road, and Billy remembered one Monday morning Joey Keane had said to him, 'Here, Billy, I seen you with your granda Saturday in town.'

Billy squeezed his eyes until the shape of the skinny conductor in his pointy shoes and the shape of Da in his sturdy hat and long winter coat drifted away.

He went back to thinking about last year, the four of them standing in Aunt Vera's porch. There'd been two tunnels of light from the headlamps of the car and the rain filled them with glittery dribbles. Behind the light they could see the shapes of the car doors opening and bits of people getting out: a foot, a shoulder, an arm, a head. Then the engine stopped and the lights went off and they couldn't see the rain any more.

Aunt Vera's voice came first. 'Good God! We thought you weren't coming. I mean, you were so late arriving and then after Maureen had rung to say she couldn't make it, well, we just presumed. And weren't we asked to a drinks party – a colleague's of Tod's up in Clonee, you know, and … Oh, this is terrible. I only hope you weren't waiting too long?'

'Ah no,' Da had begun to mutter and Billy looked down at the ground. Then Ma said, 'We got delayed and missed the first bus and we just thought seeing as we were here and that. Actually, we didn't know Maureen wasn't coming.'

The next voice he heard belonged to Mairead. 'Why didn't you just phone to say you'd be late? I mean – if you'd just phoned.'

Norman had looked up at Da, 'But we don't have a phone – do we Da?' and burst out laughing as if a phone was a mad thing to have.

Billy opened his eyes. Today the bus was mad bouncy. He tried to think of something to say to Ma. 'Is the bus bouncy because there's so few people on it?' he asked.

Ma pulled her head away from the window.

'What?'

'You know, I was thinking, maybe the more people on the bus, the less bouncy it is. Like people make it heavy and hold it down, like, near to the ground, but when there's hardly anyone on it,' he felt himself bounce again, 'it's all over the place. Would that be right, Ma?'

'Oh God, I couldn't tell you. You'd have to ask your Da something like that.' And she was gone again, back to the window.

Billy looked down the aisle. The conductor was still talking to Da, but every few seconds his eyes swivelled over to the girl and her legs. The girl kept pulling on the knot of her scarf, making the paw-marks slide from side to side, and sometimes she pulled the edge of her skirt down.

Billy watched Da. He had one hand on the bar near the platform and one foot on the step to the aisle. He could see Da just wanted to get away from the conductor's story, even though he nodded now and then and kept looking at him with his smiley eyes. He waited to see would he catch Da looking at the girl's legs. But he didn't. So after a minute he turned to look back out the window.

Soon they'd be in Clontarf. The houses were beginning to change shape, growing bigger and darker behind hedges and walls. The bigger they got, the less you could see inside. Billy thought that was the same thing as Aunt Vera's house. When you got off the bus you kept wondering where it had gone, and when you walked up the road you kept thinking you must have got off at the wrong stop because you just couldn't see it anywhere. And then suddenly there it was through the gate, standing with its porch like a room or a cave before its front door, and its tall trees going up the side, and its windows, windows, windows.

The spotty boy hadn't been in the car called Rover. The trainee pilot had been there, for once saying nothing, just climbing out of the car and standing with his hands in his pockets. After him, the boy who loved golf. But no sign of Spotty. Billy had noticed Aunt Vera lifting her eyes to an upstairs window and wondered if maybe the spotty boy had been up in his room all along. Up there, pretending not to hear the doorbell or to know they were down in the porch playing I Spy in the dark.

His face was getting hotter. Billy opened his coat and scratched the backs of his legs as hard as he could. The seat felt rough on his skin and the engine heat was drying him up so he could hardly breathe.

'Ma!' he said. 'Ma!'

Ma gave a little jump.

'When am I getting longers?'

'What?'

'Long trousers? When am I getting them?'

'I don't know – we'll see. Stop roarin', you.'

Billy glanced down the bus and decided to get as much cheek in as he could before Da came down to join them. 'Ah, you always say that – we'll see. All I want's long trousers. And I hate this jumper. It's making me all itchy.' He plucked at the jumper, crossed his arms and threw himself back on his seat.

'Listen here, you,' Ma said, 'you're nearly twelve years old, in case you didn't notice. When are you going to start acting your age?'

'I am acting me age. That's why I want long trousers.'

'For God's sake, Billy, it seems you do nothing else these days only whinge, whinge, whinge.'

'I do not!' Billy said, biting his lip and squeezing back the hot tears. He edged himself along the seat until he was looking out the opposite window to Ma's.

The last one to get out of the car had been Uncle Tod. He locked the door then walked up to the porch, lifting the side of his hands out in front of him, like he was making a frame for a picture. 'Do you know what it is?' he had said. 'Do you know now what youse remind me of standing there like that? You're like the Holy Family in the grotto there. That's what you're like.'

Tod shook the front-door key free from the bunch in his hand. He stepped up into the porch and patted Da on the arm. 'Come on, better get a drop of whiskey into this man quick now or he'll perish.'

Then he laughed and Da laughed back.

When Norman fell backwards off the seat and cracked his head like an egg on the sharp edge of the step, he didn't even cry. He whimpered a bit into Ma's coatsleeve and then just stopped. And all Billy had been able to think of was maybe now they wouldn't have to go to Aunt Vera's. He hoped it as Ma jumped up from her seat and let out a little scream, and as Da came rushing down the aisle, grabbing poles left and right to help him on his way. He hoped it even more as Ma began fussing over Norman, dusting him off and fixing his new clothes, in between hugging and kissing him.

Nobody heard the sound of the crack, only Billy.

And he wasn't always sure if he'd heard it or not. No matter how many thousands of times he went over it in his head. For all the days and for all the years that followed. And for every time he put his hand out for a bus and lifted his foot to climb on. Long after the buses had changed shape and they'd got rid of conductors and you could no longer hop on and had to wait for the doors to open. Long after the short trousers had turned into longers, the jeans with the slits in the knees had turned into suit trousers for his very first job interview. Until he had bought his own car, in fact, and never had to get on a bus again. He couldn't be certain if he'd heard the crack or if he'd imagined it.

Other things from the day would come and go, sometimes as clear as if they had only just happened, other times frayed as if they may never have happened at all. The girl with the cats' paws all over her head, the smell of the old noddy man. The silent grey sea as they turned onto the

Clontarf Road where Norman had decided to take off his coat. The sight of his bare legs up in the air. The sound of the crack.

Only one memory remained solid and true, and that was a memory that belonged to the year before. It was the picture Uncle Tod had framed in his hands. The top of the porch spiked with stars and the family inside it, lifting their arms as the headlamps lashed out, and holding their hands up to their faces, as if they were being shot in the eyes by bullets of light.

Esther's House

Since turning onto the quays I had been growing more and more anxious as the buildings and bridges continued to become more and more familiar. By the time we reached Ormond Quay Lower I was whining. Why could we not at least visit Mother, I demanded to know. Why? Why? Why?

My aunt offered me the usual excuse of Louisa's mumps.

I knew nothing about mumps except that boys my age were advised to steer well clear of them and that they were responsible for this compulsory six weeks' stay of absence, which I was now only halfway through. In any case, I thought it a bit much that I should be punished for my sister's carelessness, and just because I happened to be a boy.

'Poor Louisa,' my aunt said, 'hardly able to budge off the sofa, face up like a big balloon, God help her.'

But I saw nothing unusual in this – Louisa spent most of her time sprawled on the sofa, and she was a hefty lump besides, taking after my father for her jowly jaw. As far as I was concerned she had always had the mumps and so any sympathy I had I was keeping for myself.

The tram paused mid-quay, taunting me with a view of Capel Street, and I rushed across the aisle, kneeling up on the seat there and pressing my hands to the window. I could see the breast of my father's pub and that the cellar grid was up. I imagined Ernie down in the dark there, like the mole in the hole that he was, muttering away to himself as he went about his work, only lifting his face to the hatched light whenever a swish of dress hem passed overhead.

I looked up to the sign above the front door on the building next to the pub – *Select Accommodation for Artistic Performers. Music Rooms Available. Best Weekly Rates* – so clear I could trace the letters with my finger through the window of the tram.

This was my mother's enterprise, making use of her contacts from her old opera days – a sort of lodging house for visiting musicians. It was also where we lived.

Soft blisters of lace from the open windows – the house was taking its morning airing. Even the sash of my own bedroom window in the attic was up, and I felt the intrusion. Nobody ever bothered with my room, except for myself, and I wasn't there. I was here with Aunt Esther.

I tried to guess which window Mother was behind and what she might be doing there. Or Carolina – where would she be? Down in the back kitchen riddling the cinders. Out in the yard squeezing the guts out of newly washed linen. Up in one of the music rooms, maybe, frantically hawing a shine out of a piano.

Before I could settle on a definite picture of Carolina, the tram gong sounded and the view rattled out of my sight.

My aunt's voice came out behind me, in that slightly bewildered tone she kept for onlookers and impending scenes. 'Your mother is up to her eyes. Now be a big boy, for goodness' sake. Nursing Louisa, poor, poor Louisa. Between that and the Italians! I don't know how she –'

'What Italians?' I asked, spinning around.

'The opera company, dear – you know!'

'Nobody said anything to *me* about any opera company.'

'They're staying with your mother for the season. I told you that already.'

'No, you didn't tell me.'

'Excuse me, I did so.'

'No, you did *not* ! And how come they're not worried about catching mumps?'

My aunt leaned her face into mine, our two mouths so close then that I had to clamp my lips together to stop from swallowing her words: there would be tea later if I behaved myself, a little toy from Clery's maybe. All right, an ice-cream then in Bewley's– what do you say?

But these promises, issued through clenched teeth, sounded more like threats than treats. I shrugged my arm free from her grip.

'Oh, suit yourself then,' she snapped.

'I wish I could get away from you,' I snarled up at her.

'And I away from *you*.'

After three weeks together we had long outpassed our initial phase of politeness.

*

Every evening after supper my uncle would start the inter-rogation. I came to know his form: tongue dragging a last lick along the flat of his knife, hand pushing the plate away then returning to the back of the chair, the buttons on his park ranger's jacket jangling away until his tobacco pouch had been located.

'Well then,' he would begin, swiping his greasy fingers through his tough, gingery hair, 'so tell us – what did you get up to today?'

I never minded his questions, even the ones that he produced second time round, slyly reshaped to trip me up. Indeed, had it not been for my aunt's jittering over the crockery and cutlery I might have looked on this time of the day as a welcome half hour of conversation. There was little else in the way of company for me here; my aunt or the cats were the size of it. And I hated the cats: their foolish names and pissy smell, the way they were always on the make for a scrap of food or the warmth of a recently vacated bed, armchair or coat left on the sofa. Their mechanical purring and deranged night-time crying, the presumptuous way they rubbed themselves off your leg: I hated their very nature.

Whatever it was that my uncle was after with his questions was still, at this stage, unclear to me, although it was obvious that Chapelizod Bridge – or something on the far side of it – had some significance, for all questions seemed to come to the bridge: had I seen it, had we crossed over it, did I notice the shop on the other side, what about that mad skinny oulone in the bockity house on the way up to the next village, hanging over the half-door like a horse all day?

I had often heard it said by Carolina that my aunt's 'little peculiarities' were down to the bad match she had made.

'She could have had anyone,' according to Carolina, 'anyone! With her face and figure and that voice like an angel. Pity she didn't take a leaf out of your mother's much-more-sensible book.'

But I saw little difference between the two husbands. Except for my uncle's colouring and brambled beard, they were even similar in appearance. Both were quiet men, not easily lured into conversation – although my father could manage pub banter well enough, or at least roll out the same few sentences all day long for the benefit of each new customer. Both men ate with their faces close to the plate and thought nothing of belching or scratching in public.

If anything, I found my uncle to be the gentler of the two, his presence much less demanding. And at least he would talk to me – first thing in the morning while it was still nearly dark and he was fumbling around making his lunch or eating his breakfast. Or if I came across him out in the garden, sitting on a log in fine weather or in the outhouse when it was raining where he would eat his sandwiches, as if he were miles away from his own kitchen table. And a few times when he took me with him on his rounds. On those occasions he would nearly always ask me about my father's business.

So how is your oulfella doing these days – raking it in, I don't doubt?

How many has he working for him now – a right houseful, I suppose?

Does the pub be busy – packed to the gills, I'm sure?

Would you say he did well for himself – he certainly did, all considered?

As he tended to answer the questions himself, there wasn't too much for me to do on these chats, but I enjoyed them just the same.

*

Every time I left my aunt's house the daylight always came as a shock – the size of the sky. I was used to a dark house, for we lived on one of the darkest streets in the city. But the darkness in my aunt's house was different. The house was set on the hump of a hill at the side of the Fifteen Acres in the Phoenix Park, surrounded by an inner circle of dark-green railings and an outer circle of trees. There was no shortage of windows, there was even an ill-named sunroom that bellied out onto the garden – yet somehow the light always seemed to be skulking outside as if it were afraid to come in.

This day my aunt was even more agitated than usual – she forgot to feed the cats and I didn't bother to remind her. She kept walking in and out of rooms until finally she told me to put on my coat, cap and boots. Keeping a hard hold of my hand, she dragged me all the way down the hill from the house, never letting go, even as she shoved us clumsily through the turnstile gate into Park Lane. Her step remained brisk until we came to the village, and then it slowed up. I could feel the effort this cost her.

'We're just going as far as the bridge to give this little chap a look at the swans, as far as the bridge I told to him, but no further, for he'll give me no peace till he sees the swans.' This was the announcement she made to anyone we happened to pass: the greengrocer struggling with his awning; the group waiting at the bus stop; the nurse pushing a baby's pram from one of the grander houses that led up to the Knockmaroon hill and the Strawberry Beds. All had to hear about the swans, and all seemed to be slightly embarrassed by the news. It was almost as if she was asking their permission.

I had never really noticed anything odd in my aunt's behaviour until I came to stay with her, apart from the fact that when she came on a visit to our house she couldn't seem to stop talking. My mother said this was because she was lonely and that it wouldn't kill us to indulge her a little with the occasional nod or reply. Which we did, often for what seemed like hours on end, my aunt chattering away about little or nothing while the tea grew cold in the pot and a skin grew over the jam.

In her own house she rarely spoke. She spent a lot of time looking in the mirror too – not the way my mother would do, with some sense of purpose, to fix her hair or rouge up her cheeks and sigh discontentedly at some aspect of her appearance. Aunt Esther just stared at herself as if she were studying a picture of a stranger. And she was so gentle – in movements as well as in voice. Yet she played the piano with something like violence. If a knock came to the door she wouldn't answer it but came looking for me to do so, even if I was out in the garden or already asleep in bed. And now there was this business of lying to strangers about my wanting to see the swans.

We got to the bridge, and my aunt tugged me over it so sharply that I saw nothing of the swans and nothing of the river other than one section of water with the light wriggling on it like hundreds of worms.

'But what about the swans?'

'On the way back.'

It was a long trek all uphill after that and far too warm for October. Pinned by the sun to a high stone wall that seemed to have no intention of ending, I struggled behind my aunt, heels dragging, sweaty body wriggling against my coat, head boiling under my cap.

I sent up several long sighs of distress but my aunt appeared not to notice.

At last a stretch of railing broke into the wall, then a gate flanked by two tall round pillars. Here we stopped. And still she said nothing.

I looked up at the sign arched over the gate but it was too high up to see properly.

'It says "Stewarts Hospital for Imbecile Children",' my aunt whispered then.

I recognised the word 'imbecile', having heard my father use it often enough to his bar staff and was curious to see how this might apply to children. My aunt pushed me towards the gate.

She tucked herself in behind a pillar, her back to the railings, a handkerchief muffling her mouth as if she'd been appalled by a sudden smell. Then she shoved me into position at the gate.

I could barely hear her instructions.

'What do you see?'

'Nothing.'

'You must see something?'

'Well, there's trees, a bench, a big building, a sort of verandah.'

'Step closer. Now. Can you see any people? People?'

'A sick-nurse?'

'Yes, a nurse. Good, that's good. Anyone else?'

'Two more nurses.'

'And? Come on, and?'

'Well …'

'Who? Who?'

'Sick people … I suppose.'

'Is there a boy there?'

'Yes. There's a few.'

'Red hair. He'll have red hair. Well? Answer me – won't you answer me? Is he? Is he there?'

'I don't know. How old is he?'

'Fifteen. Can you see him?'

'Yes. Yes, I think so. At least he's the only one with red hair.'

We caught the tram home and she never opened her mouth, handing me the money to pay for the fare. As the tram crossed back over Chapelizod Bridge I looked out the window, but saw no swans on the river.

We pushed through the turnstile gate back into the park and she started to sob and sobbed all the way up the hill. When we got into the house she was still at it, standing in the centre of the sunroom, as if her whole face were weeping, her mouth, her nose, her eyes.

'Oh my God,' she said, 'if your uncle ever finds out. If he ever finds out …'

A few minutes later she called out from her bedroom for a glass of water and a small green bottle that I would find under the spools in her sewing basket.

I held the glass while she sipped. She was still crying although the sobs were smoother now. After a while they stopped altogether. Then she pulled back the eiderdown and asked me to get in beside her.

I started to fidget, mumbled something about lessons, the amount of school I was missing, the promises I had made to Mother to keep up my singing exercises. But my aunt was having none of it. 'I'm so cold,' she said, 'so very cold.'

Then I came up with the excuse of feeding the cats.

'Just a few little minutes,' she pleaded, her voice slow and sleepy, 'that's all I ask.'

I fed the cats. When I came back in, she was waiting. I took my time in unlacing my boots and longer still to take off my socks. When I had finished her eyes were still open.

I lay with my back to her, trapped by her arms, and her smells, which up to now had only come in loose passing hints, were wrapped like swaddling around me: rosewater and dress-sweat; a sour, dry aroma that reminded me of a bonfire after all the heat had gone out of it.

My body stiff as a plank, hers soft and full as pillows behind me. Whispers tipped off the back of my neck and nestled like nits in my hair; senseless whispers about secrets and babies and promises never to tell.

Toby, she said the boy's name was, fifteen last May, same age as Louisa, bar a few months.

I closed my eyes and thought of the ginger boy and all the lies I had told her about him. He's reading a book, I had said, now smiling at the nurse, now talking to a boy at his side.

When I woke up there was only the sound of her sleeping breath.

I slid out of bed then took my boots to the sunroom. But the sunroom was too close to her room and no corner of the house seemed to be far enough. I put on my boots, walked through the garden and stood at the side of the Fifteen Acres.

Such an amount of sky! A big black skin of sky, and the stars on it like a rash of silver scabs.

*

I painted a picture for Mother. Taking my time with it, stroke by careful stroke, patiently waiting for each colour to dry before adding the next. My uncle set up the easel and brought me the paints. Sometimes standing next to me, telling me what to do, and I could see that his hand longed to take the brush off me, but in the end it just hovered and I did it myself. He told me how to apply colour. How to blot it off again when I made a mistake.

The picture shows my Aunt Esther's house and all the trees that surround it: dark, curly evergreens and the spindly brown bones of those in full moult. The Dublin Mountains are mauve in the background; there's the dip of Chapelizod Village: yellow and red, a line of rooftops peeping over the dark grey wall of the Phoenix Park.

The deer I have relocated from the far side of the Acres where they sleep in their little scoops. Now they sleep on the hill beside the house. Instead I've put them sleeping on the hill beside the house. It's a bit of a cheat, but my uncle said it's all right to cheat for the sake of the picture and that he doubted the deer would mind. My uncle knows the deer so well that when he strolls through the middle of the herd they don't scatter but lift their sturdy necks and, with their black steady eyes, watch him pass by.

When I've finished the picture I make my signature in the corner so Mother will always know who it came from. My uncle puts a frame around it, then wraps it in four sheets of crisp brown paper. I call my picture *Esther's House*. My uncle says it's a very good name, although strictly speaking the house is his.

It helps me to put in the days of the last two weeks of my stay.

And in the evenings I sit by my aunt while she bashes the piano. This is after we have gone to see the boy and are up and out of our afternoon bed. I used to turn the pages for her, but I stopped doing that ages ago. She never looks at the music anyway.

While she plays I am walking myself in my mind through our house in Capel Street. I can see Mother and Carolina then, as they are at this hour of the day when it's time to put the lights on so the guests can see as they climb up the stairs. I follow them both as they move through the house, room by room, corner by corner, flight by flight. Everywhere they go they leave light behind.

*

When I get home only Ernie is there. He tells me Mother has gone out and that I've only just missed her. 'Gone to the train station to see off them bloody Eyeties – doubt she'll be back for a while yet. A swank tea they were having before setting off. In the Shelbourne, or maybe she said some place else.'

Then he tells me Father is with his bookkeeper and he's not to be disturbed. But there's no need for him to tell me this, as I have no intention of disturbing my father and hadn't asked for him in the first place.

'Your sister is up in the sitting-room.'

'Where's Carolina?'

'Day off.'

I go up to Mother's bedroom thinking I'll leave the picture there for a surprise, maybe hide myself behind the curtain until she finds it, pick the right moment before popping out: 'Sur-priiiiise!'

This plan makes me so giddy I nearly trip up the stairs.

But there's no place for the picture in Mother's room. The bed is bumpy and bright with laid-out clothes she has been trying on. Her dressing table packed with little bottles and boxes. The mantel over the fireplace crowded with cards and ornaments. Hat boxes all over the floor. I try leaning the picture against the wardrobe door, but it slides off the mahogany surface.

There's a funny smell in the bedroom. The vaguely farty smell of my father is gone and there's a new sweet smell that I don't recognise – oranges and perfume maybe. There are things in the room I've never seen either, vases stuffed up with flowers and a neat, fat bunch of Parma violets lying on the chair. A box of figs is open on the floor. Sorrento figs, so the lid says. There's a man's photograph poked into the corner of the dressing mirror – a profile I've never met, a deep black signature scrawled over one shoulder.

In the end I just leave my picture on the floor then go to the window and pull the curtains around me.

The window pane holds a glaze of my face, dark and devilish. It shows years I haven't yet lived, scars I haven't yet earned. It shows every minute of every day of the last six weeks of my life.

A ginger-haired boy and sneery-eyed cats. A broken body slumped in a wheelchair. The shape of my aunt's bed and my boots on the floor. My uncle wading through a far-off herd of deer.

These are the images that fill up my reflection, edging in and out, swelling and shrinking, melting into my face, my arms, my chest.

Windows of Eyes

The girl forced her hands up out of her pockets, then further up to the back of her neck. Clutching the collar of her gabardine coat, they drew it up as far as it would go. She wished she hadn't cut her hair now; her hair could have acted as a sort of a sponge against the rain and the back of her neck wouldn't have to feel like a damp concrete block.

She turned into Castlewood Avenue, taking the slip lane off it then moving into the cutaway that led past the cottages. She had covered these streets already today, scuttling with them from Ballsbridge to here. Tight little corners and squashed-in cottages; back-lane entrances to the big houses out on the avenue. Barely enough room for a car to pass through, no fear of a bus with its windows of eyes.

Maybe it would look different now, going the opposite way, on the opposite side of the road. Maybe it would look different in the dark. But apart from a rare piddle of light from an upstairs window it was the same. Same rain-stained walls; same broken bin outside same banjaxed garage door. The sky was a different colour now, that was all.

Hands shaking. She watched them under a pyramid of streetlight switch coins from one to another. There was a fiver still in her pencil-case and four cigarettes left in the box: that was her lot. On her palm just about enough coins to pay for a newspaper and a lighter – neither of which was really necessary. But the thoughts of having to ask a stranger on the street for a light. And the thoughts, too, of sitting in a café without a newspaper to hide behind. There were books in her bag – plenty of books – but she didn't want to be reminded of school or of tomorrow, and she didn't want either to look like a schoolgirl alone in a late-night café. She came out of the cutaway and onto Mount Pleasant Avenue.

Window after blindfolded window. Houses cut up into makey-up homes, a cluster of bells to a door. Not a human in sight. Cars, though, as far as the eye could see, snout to tail, on both sides of the road. Cars sleek with rain and streetlight. There was something beautiful in the sturdy, rain-polished shape of them and the promise, too, of their dry, soft interiors. One careless driver – that's all it would take – one door left unlocked out of so many. She could come back to it later, after the café, slip in, lock the door safely behind her. Some cars even had rugs in them. Plaid hairy rugs – you'd often see them folded on a shelf at the back window. She could curl up on the floor, turn herself into a plaid hairy parcel. But she would need to be gone before daylight and what if she slept it out? Or worse, what if the owner was a shift worker, a nurse or a postman maybe, someone who started the day before the night was even over? There was no way of knowing. If she lived along here, she might have some idea of who owned which car and what time they set off. The Mondeo man with the briefcase on the dot of seven. The dental receptionist who hopped into her Mini Cooper at a quarter-past eight. But she didn't live here; her house was away from here. Fifteen bus stops away and not far enough at that.

She decided to forget about the cars, about where or how she would sleep. Step by step was enough for the moment. Step by step, the next cigarette and soon the café.

She came to a pub on a corner. A curve of warm yellow light from a big bay window. Inside, dancing shapes in a television high up on the wall. The back view of a man looking up at it, one hand stretched towards his pint on the counter, the other on his hip. The slow, lazy movement of a nearby barman. At a table just inside the window, a young man – not all that much older than herself – was staring out at her. Why was he staring? He nudged his companion who turned, stood up and leaned in to the window, placing the palms of his hands on the glass and making a face. Jeering at her. Why was he jeering at her? She realised then that she'd been staring in – how long had she been staring in? – and that's why they were staring out. Cheeks burning, she hurried away. Cold rain smacked her face, gradually replacing the heat with a painful tingle.

At the top of the avenue she could see the main road; only a few cars passing now, silent intervals between them. A short while ago when she'd passed this way it was still bright enough to see by; she hadn't been able to hear the silence then for the sound of car engines snipping by. On the far side of the road, a strip of dark grass, the big, raggy heads on an alley of trees, the pathway, canal bank; behind all that, canal water.

On the bank looking down, she stood for a while watching the rain pluck at the skin of green water. She could see the hooked neck of a swan in the shadow under the bridge and hear a purr of music from one of the pubs on the street above. On the opposite bank, a man in a tracksuit running under trees lifted his hands and jabbed punches on the air: double right, triple left, double right again. The quarter chime from the town-hall clock came out of nowhere, startling her. She couldn't seem to remember which quarter it was – to or past? Maybe half-past then? But half-past what though? Ten? Eleven?

One cigarette per hour: that was the deal she had made with herself. After four cigarettes, it would be time to eat. How many had she smoked so far? Now she was all mixed up. Numbers and chimes rattled inside her head, the nuts and bolts of lost time. After all the hours of nursing the minutes, adding them up, reining them in. After all that, and she couldn't even remember.

She turned from the canal bank and made for the road. A car was parked at the edge, a man's half-face looking out over a half-mast window. He said something to her. Something she couldn't quite catch. She stepped into the streetlight. 'Sorry, I didn't hear – what?'

The man moved his hand as if to swat her away. 'Ah, forget it,' he said, the window gliding up as he drove away.

It would get brighter, she told herself, the further she walked, the closer she came to Rathmines centre. The town hall clock was lit up anyway, lit up like a big, fat moon scratched with numbers, returning the time to her. A quarter to eleven. She could see the dome of the church now, a giant military helmet on a big, swollen head, peering awkwardly over the rooftops.

Across the road was a square – a playing field, really, black trees and black grass. Railings. She considered going over to it, looking for a space to squeeze through, maybe find a spot in the bushes where she could make a nest for later on. But the dark seemed solid over there, the road too wide to cross, and her legs were too heavy and sore to do anything other than move in a straight, long line.

Almost at the church now, she wondered about going inside. She could sit on a dry seat anyway. Light a candle, hold her hands over the nip of its sharp little flame. Pretend to put money in the slot.

But there would be no sound to confirm that a coin had dropped and someone might notice. She could count the statues then, study their faces. If she did go in, it would be her second time that day and what if the same priest was in there pottering around? He'd wonder what she was at. He might ask if she wanted confession. He might think she had some sort of a vocation and want to talk to her about God. Or he might ask other questions. What was her name and where did she live and did her mother know she was out so late on her own? He might – no, he would – recognise the school uniform.

She came to the gates, stopped and peered through the railings, past the pillars and the portico. The long iron doors locked for the night. No need to worry, so, about the coins or the priest and his questions.

Further along. She stopped to look back: a bus in the distance, familiar number, sharpening into focus. She turned her face to the window of an empty shop; the bus stalled behind her, sighed then screeched off again, dragging a jagged reflection of light across the glass: bare shelves and old letters, torn posters, dust.

In Londis, people were buying small: small sliced pans, small cartons of milk. You could get twin sausages wrapped in cellophane. You could buy one egg. There were men in the queue with cement-dusted boots and a gypsy woman wearing chubby pink runners. under a long yellow and green skirt. She bought an evening paper and the smallest green lighter, dropping her money into the cupped brown hand of the shop assistant.

In the doorway of a charity shop, she turned the lighter over in her hand and waited for the hour to chime. The window display held its own story: an old-fashioned evening bag and a bookcase of books. There were candlesticks and a lamp, a spotty dress on a headless dummy. A long mirror on a stand.

The hour sounded; chimes blossomed and fell all over Rathmines.

The side of the long mirror showed a reflection: pale hands moving through a tangle of smoke; cigarette tip floating to and from an unseen mouth, watched by unseen eyes. Almost done – one more pull and the cigarette would be past the golden ring. One half a pull then it would be over. She came outside. The rain had stopped.

There was a palm tree painted on the sign above the café and the words *Sunset Strip Café* written in a slant beside it. She remembered when she was small her older cousin telling her that this was a rude place where women took off their clothes and men whistled loudly. For years she had believed that.

She pushed the door in. Glass smeared with fog and long trickles of condensation made it look as if it was raining on the inside. A blurt of greasy hot steam on her face making her feel sick and hungry all at once. The sting of fluorescent light in her eyes; she waited for the blots and squiggles to clear then closed the door behind her.

A thin figure in pink polyester was clattering behind the counter. Scant hair tied at the back, black eyeliner. One eyebrow lifted as if to say: Well, what do you want?

Her order stumbled out and the waitress quickly caught it. It seemed like only seconds before a cup and saucer landed on the counter, followed by a Pyrex plate with a slice of bread cut on the diagonal, the bread already buttered or, more likely, margarined.

The café was long and narrow: rows of tables cut by two long, narrow aisles. At the back wall, a pair of toilet doors: silhouette of a top-hatted gent on one; lady-in-waiting on the other. Across the ranks, single occupants zig-zagged, one to a table. Somewhere near the toilets would be best; she could drop her stuff under the table and duck inside, steep her hands in hot, hot water; stoop her head under the hand dryer just to feel the blast of scorching air on the back of her neck. But it was a long trek to the end of the café with her bag dragging down on one shoulder and the freezing fingers of both hands trying to keep a grip on the plate as well as the cup and saucer. She felt a weakness in her wrists, and the sudden heat was drawing a long, watery snot from one nostril.

She slid into the nearest seat, her hand, the cup and saucer chattering like a set of minute teeth. She slid into the nearest seat. Releasing the bag from her shoulder, she let it slide down on the floor then pulled a napkin from the dispenser on the wall and dabbed at her nose. She began plucking out other napkins, furtively stuffing them down into her pocket for later.

The man sitting opposite had his evening paper perched on the cruet set. He shifted the paper a few inches to the right, but otherwise gave no sign that he'd noticed her. He was eating a mixed grill, moving the food around as he ate so that she kept catching rotating glimpses of his meal: the nub of a sausage, a rasher rind, a dab of egg yolk, black pudding. Ramming the lumps into his mouth, slurping on the tea, topping it up from a large pot here and there, he reached and chewed and sawed and lifted. His eyes never left his newspaper.

She had to return to the counter for a knife and fork. When she came back he shifted his newspaper a little to the right again, as if he'd forgotten he'd already done that, or as if he thought she had been and gone and was now being replaced by somebody else.

The waitress came over carrying a side plate of chips and a small pot of tea. Is that your lot? her smudged eyes seemed to say. She put the bill on the table, trapping it under a vinegar bottle.

The chips felt hard in her mouth; hard and tainted with old oil. There was no pleasure to be had from them and yet she had to control the urge to wolf them down. There was a sort of yearning in the pit of her stomach, and in her throat a compulsive gulping. In her mind she whispered: 'Slow down, slow down, slow down. Make it last.'

There was nowhere to put her own newspaper; the man opposite was taking all the space. It had been a waste to buy it. She glanced at the bill – cheaper than she had expected it to be. Had she not bothered with the paper she could have afforded more: chips on a bigger plate, an egg maybe.

She looked down the café. All the tables occupied by men. Repeats of the man at her table. Newspapers and mixed grills – a trick with mirrors. A table to the side had just become vacant, but she felt that somehow it would be bad manners to move to it now. Not that the man opposite her would notice or care. But the waitress would. Closing time soon: she could see it in the waitress's tired, fluorescent-lit face and in the territorial way her eye had just dropped on the recently vacated table.

Almost finished. Her hand reached for the last chip. No more than a couple of bites left on the slice of bread. The tea nearly gone. Soon the waitress would have the lot whipped away from her and she'd be back out on the street. She lifted the teapot and shook out the last drop. All the hours that had been leading up to this. All the quarter-hours she'd built out of minutes just to cross them off in her head. To bring her that bit closer to here. To this lukewarm tea, to these few hard chips, this slice of stale bread. This notion of warmth in her belly, on her face, the flat of her hand when she patted the teapot. Now it was nearly over. And after this, what?

The man opposite stood up sharply, the legs of his chair like claws scraping along the floor. He rolled his paper, stuck it into his jacket pocket then collected his bits: keys, pen, a folded tweed cap. He took a step away then came back for the bill, stretching over the table and leaving behind him a yeasty whiff of beer and egg. His eye rims were raw, she noticed.

She looked down at the remains on his plate. A scatter of chips stained with ketchup; a chop that needed handling in order to be finished; a sausage; two dark turdish pieces of liver. It was the sausage in its entirety that got to her. Thick, brown, glistening. Uncut.

Her hand made a few cautious moves in the direction of the plate. Once it even touched the rim, but immediately withdrew. She lifted the empty cup to her lips and pretended to drink. For a few seconds she bit her thumbnail. Then the hand went down again and this time it landed.

Cold sausage meat, clammy on the roof of her mouth, rubbery and stubborn. She chewed on, jaws frantically clicking, elbows resting on the table, hands fanned over her face. The ping of a cash register behind her and the man, cap on head, already passing by the window outside.

The waitress was beside her now, hand quick as a fish darting through the debris on the table, pulling things to one side, flicking a cloth in between. She didn't have to look up to know she'd been caught in the act; the warm mess sitting like something alive in her mouth.

Her hand reached down, lifted the flaps of her schoolbag, dipped in and patted around till the pencil case was located. Her fingers pulled the fiver out and left it with the bill on the table, she couldn't make herself wait for the change, nor could she even think about walking all the way down the aisle to get to the toilets.

Damp coat slapping on the back of her legs, she moved quickly along the now-deserted street. She turned a corner, crossed the road, veered into the laneway off Castlewood Avenue, back again to where she had started. She took the napkin out of her pocket and spread it out in both hands, a picture of a tiny palm tree in one corner. Opening her mouth as wide as a lion, she pushed out her tongue and let the mess drop down into the napkin: meat, gristle, a few slips of sausage skin, her own warm, sour spit.

The girl remembered then, the large, fat fingers of the man and the way the dirt of the day, or maybe even days, had been lodged into the creases in his knuckles and smeared on the cuff of his shirtsleeves and under his fingernails in slender black arches.

Bridie's Wedding

Brim to brim across the hall table, hats laid out like puddings in a cake shop. On the floor, a geometry of different shaped parcels. Each one wears a tight skin of coloured paper and a little tag of identification: Arnotts, Switzers, Guineys, Clerys. But she is not tempted, not today, to slip a fingernail where it should not be and tear a sneaky peek-gap. Today she has urgent news. More urgent even than Bridie's wedding. She must find Mother. But first she must find a space for her schoolbag.

Out of the hall and into the front parlour: flowers all over the place. Resting in bouquets on the floor, standing in little pots of water against the wall, turning the room into an indoor garden for the eve of Bridie's wedding. Vera's foot swings from a ladder and her hand presses a frame of blooms around the mantelpiece mirror. Maureen leans her weight on the end of the ladder, her face all agitated, her mouth moving even before it begins to speak. 'What are you gawking at? The piano needs polishing.'

'I'm looking for Mother.'

'Can you see her in here – can you? No? Then go. And get that bloody bag out of here.'

Outside again, and now through the second door into the back parlour. Jack is making a table out of boards and Charlie sits on the edge of the sofa, bent over a tin of nails, his fingers trickling through them like they were water.

A blotch-faced Bridie stands in the corner, pressing starch into sheets.

'What's wrong, Bridie? Are you crying? What's wrong with Bridie? Is she crying? Bridie – what?'

'You mind your own business,' Jack says.

'If you tell anyone about the chocolates,' Bridie sniffs, 'I'll kill you.'

'Tell what?' she asks. 'Tell what about the chocolates? How can I tell if I don't even…?'

'Out,' Bridie and Jack say together. Charlie says nothing, but just for a moment his fingers stop moving.

'Can I leave my bag in here for a while?'

'No!'

And that's how it's been for the bag and for her these past few days, being shooed from room to room like a pair of old chickens. Nowhere to go except into the next room or down to the shops on a message. And it seems to her a little odd that up to this and Bridie's wedding no one even knew what colour her bag was. And now it has become the household pest. For a while it had seemed easier just to keep it on her back until it was time for bed, but Kay said that would just be asking for a hump.

And where's Mother, she wonders, sitting herself and the bag at the end of the stairs. I have to find Mother.

Mr Clifford's voice comes down the stairs and hovers over her head. Leaning back, she can see his legs in their pinstripe trousers, growing out of the step at the top of the first landing and, above them, the silver loop of his watch chain against the dim light. His arms hang by his side; a newspaper flops from one hand.

'You can leave the bag in my room,' he says.

'I'll have to ask Mother,' she begins, but already he's disappeared up to his room on the second landing.

Mr Clifford is the opposite to her and her bag. He's the lodger and cannot be upset. Mr Clifford always comes first. 'Good money, that's the why,' is what Maureen always says any time she asks the question.

She skips down the basement stairs and into the scullery, pulling back the long draught-curtain. Eileen standing at the sink, a cloth in one hand, a small brown chocolate in the other. Carefully she pats it, before laying it back down into its nest at the bottom of the chocolate box.

'What are you doing, Eileen, with the –?'

'I'm dusting the chocolates.'

'Why?'

'Because I feel like it.'

She walks backwards into the kitchen. 'Oh, Mother,' she gasps, 'oh, thank God you're here.'

'Where else would I be?' Mother says.

'Eileen is dusting the chocolates …'

'Yes.'

Mother sits at a table with a big fat white turkey on her lap, viciously picking at stuck stalks of feathers. There's a lump of raw ham squeezed into a big pot and strands of uncooked sausages in a soft grey plait on a plate. A bolster of dark-red beef sits on another plate. Under the pepper pot the bloodstained bill from Costelloe's butcher's is covered in little sums.

Mother rolls her sleeves up and slaps the turkey on the bottom before placing it on a dish. She clicks her fingers now and then at a fly swaying over her head.

'Such news, Mother. You'll never guess what?'

'Don't tell me you're getting married now.'

'Oh no. But when I do, I'll have it in a hotel. So you won't have to pay Costelloe's not one single penny.'

Mother half smiles. 'Good girl.'

She hoists the schoolbag off her back and slides her hand into the pocket on the front, careful not to graze her knuckles on the catch hiding inside. She hands the note to Mother and waits.

Mother's pinny is a navy-blue sky, flicked with hundreds of stars. She wipes the meat stains on the front of it and takes the note, unfolding it slowly. She sits down then and 'Oh God, that's all I need now. That's all.'

Mother lays the note down on her lap and she is quiet, too quiet for a long time.

'What's she done now?' Maureen asks, barrelling into the kitchen, a stack of folded napkins held like a melodeon between her hands.

'Nothing. But nothing. I can't see the blackboard and ...'

'She needs glasses,' Mother says at last.

'Yes. The nurse says I have to.'

'Is that all?' Maureen laughs, glances at Mother then takes a step back and stops. 'Can't she get them on the scheme, Mother?'

But she doesn't want them on the scheme. She wants Mother to pay for them. If she gets them on the scheme everyone will know. Those awful pink frames, that plastic case. Why, it might as well have *pauper* printed on it. She wants ones like Millicent Greene has. Gliding up at the hinge to one small but elegant diamond. And a special yellow cloth like a tiny desk duster, folded neatly into a box with a proper optician's name engraved under the lid. A box that's blue, maybe, and hard as a suitcase. A box that goes *clop* when you close it, nearly biting the fingers off you.

If she can't have long hair, or lemonade in its own bottle instead of milk from an old whiskey 'baby', and if she can't have a single stitch that's not been pared down from her sisters – well, why can't she at least have glasses like Milly Greene's?

'Mother,' says Maureen, 'are you listening to me now? She can get them for nothing on the Widows and Orphans. You won't have to pay. Don't give in to her. Don't.'

But Mother stands up; her lips squeeze in and say, 'We'll manage …'

And that's all she needs to hear.

She hugs Mother, whispers a thank you and her face feels a cold pinch from the nappy pins Mother still wears on the breast of her apron even though there hasn't been a baby in this house for years.

'I'll polish the piano,' she says, running off.

'Come back here, Miss,' Mother calls. 'What about your bag?'

'Oh, Mr Clifford said I could leave it in his room – is that all right?'

Mother nods. 'Take it up so. And ask him if he could have his tea on a tray, just for this once.'

'Yes, Mother.'

'And ask nicely, mind.'

'Oh yes, Mother.

On the top landing, she knocks at his door. Above her the skylight is the colour of jewels: red ruby, amethyst, sapphire blue, emerald. Her eyes stay on it even after his 'Yessss …'

His dressing-gown swings on the back of the door; a fawn thing with roped stitching. It makes her think of the dressing-gown her father had when he was sick, the same but different, hanging on this very door when this used to be his room where he slept with Mother before he died and Mr Clifford became their lodger.

'My bag, Mister Clifford,' she says. 'I asked Mother. And, and you said before that if I …? My bag.'

He points to a space beside where he stands. A space that seems a long way off. She crosses the room, taking care not to appear nosey by looking around but at the same time managing to notice – the good yellow chair from the front parlour, the radio that used to be in the kitchen, the statue of the shepherd boy from the hall.

She places the bag on the ground beside him and slowly he heels it under the bed. His hand comes down and pats her head. Then it moves as if it's looking for somewhere to land. It pauses before settling on her shoulder. 'Pretty thing,' he says, 'pretty dress.' He smiles at her with all his teeth. She can't see his eyes behind his glinty glasses.

'Oh and … Excuse me please, Mister Clifford, Mother says. Mother says, she hopes you don't mind tea on a tray. Just for this once. Again.'

Mr Clifford nods.

Downstairs in the hall Maureen is waiting. 'Mister Clifford thinks my uniform is pretty,' she whispers to Maureen, laughing under her breath. 'Don't you think that's funny? A school uniform? Pretty!'

But Maureen doesn't answer her. She pushes her, though, straight into the front parlour where Kay looks up from a list in her hand.

'Tell her you don't want them. Tell her you don't mind,' Maureen says.

'Tell who? Mind what?'

'You know fine well what and who. The glasses. Do you know how long I was saving to pay for my outfit tomorrow? Do you have any idea?'

She doesn't know. She knows, however, that it's best to keep your mouth shut when Maureen is angry. Best to pretend to listen and to think about something else.

'She can't afford it. *We* can't afford it.'

'Well, Mother said I could. She said, she said –'

'Oh, well for you all right and the rest of us working to pay for your notions.'

Maureen pinches her arm.

'Owww!'

'Oh, leave her be,' Kay says, 'what difference is it going to make now? '

Maureen goes out and slams the door and the cards on the mantelpiece shudder. She waits to hear which way Maureen has gone. Upstairs. First landing. Bathroom.

'Kay? Kay, what am I not supposed to tell about the chocolates?'

'Old Clifford's chocolates? Oh, there's nothing to tell.'

'Has it something to do with Eddie?' she asks, because all secret things have Eddie behind them.

'Forget about the chocolates. Just don't eat any tomorrow.'

'Ah … That's not fair. Why not?'

'Because. They're won't be enough to go round all the guests, we've all agreed….'

'Oh. But why did they make Bridie cry?'

'Weddings always make people cry.'

'Then why do they have them?'

Vera's eyes smile and her eyebrow gives a little shrug.

*

Bridie sits on the windowsill sipping hot milk and turmeric. Maureen sits by her side hugging her knees. From over the top of the bedclothes she can see bits of her two eldest sisters: the orange streetlight all over their nighties, their heads stuffed with curlers. Their whispers stay with them in the bay of the window, but the odd one strays across the room and delicious it is when it's caught. Bridie is afraid of something, something to do with Joe.

And Maureen? Maureen is thrilled by the same something that Bridie is afraid of. But who could be scared of Joe? His slanty smile and Adam's apple like a small, bouncy ball in his neck.

She wonders has it do with being in your nude? Milly says when you get married you have to go to bed in your nude. But Bridie would never do that. Why even in here, in front of her own sisters, she would unpeel herself under her nightdress as if she were an orange in a circus. Afraid of Joe! Harmless old Joe. Poor old Joe, Mother always says.

*

Meat sweat sneaks up the stairs and wakes her. The smell of cooking so early. She opens her eyes and the room is alive. With crispy dress cloth and hairspray hissing and stockings slapping into place. And Bridie's face like a small white turnip through the mirror and then changing slowly with each pat of colour into a bride for Joe.

'I'm bursting,' she says to anyone who is listening, and Maureen says, 'Well, you'll just have to wait. Sir Clifford is in there.'

And so she lies back and waits, nursing the urge.

Eileen says, 'Quick, he's finished,' and they all stop to listen to the cough that he always gives when he comes out of the bathroom.

He's left the smell of himself inside, so she holds her nose and tries not to breathe. He's left the heat of himself as well round the rim of the toilet seat. And some dead black hairs stuck in the lump of foam on his shaving mirror. She makes two circles from her fingers and places them over her eyes before she looks in. Just to give her face a practice for when she gets her new glasses.

Back in the bedroom, Kay helps her to dress, guiding her frock down over her arms and playing the skirt until it stands stiff and wide. There's a netted petticoat underneath that pushes it into shape, and a thin fall of peach satin over that. The neckline is trimmed with tiny cloth roses. Kay ties her sash and flicks out the bow then slowly turns her towards the mirror

'Now,' she says, 'what do you see?'

'Oh, Kay ... I'm so ...'

She nearly says I'm so lovely, but remembers what Mother said about being too full of herself.

'It's so lovely, Kay. *It's* so ...'

*

Eddie says he'll walk back from North William Street Church because there isn't enough room in the car. But there is. Right here beside her. She tries to tell him. But he doesn't seem to hear. And even though he walks away, hands in his pockets, eyes watching his own feet as if he doesn't know which way they'll be going, she sits the same way, her dress bunched up into a lump on her lap. So that Eddie's space stays vacant all the way home.

Inside the house now and so many people, they all seem to know her even though she doesn't know the half of them.

Jack comes up the brown scullery stairs, a tray held high, shouting his head off.

'Load coming through, gangway, gangway! The management will not be responsible.'

And one of the aunties laughs and says he's a scream.

There's sherry and port for the ladies, Kay explains to her, and stout for the men and whiskey, only if they ask. Or if Mother says. She nods and goes around group to group taking orders and bringing them back to Charlie, who slaps a teacloth over his shoulder and stares into each glass as it grows its own colour from stem to brim. Bridie's cheeks are stained with prints of strange kisses and Joe stands by her side shaking all hands and grinning out of his big red face. The tray with the meat comes up the stairs all cooked and juicy, and Mr Costelloe looks down at it, grinning approval and telling everyone that it's come from his shop. 'You'd think he was after giving it to us for nothing,' she hears Maureen mutter to Kay.

And everyone says that her dress is so pretty and that she won't feel it now till she's getting married herself and twirl after twirl is called for until her head gets too dizzy. Mister Clifford sips whiskey in the corner and says nothing.

She stops for a minute and looks all around, trying to understand the shape of the room. The partition doors between the two parlours have been unscrewed from the walls and the table that Jack made yesterday is a bridge between them, with the sheets Bridie pressed pretending to be tablecloths, like snow on the ground. Platters of sliced ham at its centre and all around it pots of cream and butter, mustard and horseradish. There's hills of bread rolls and brown sausages. Skinned scallions sprout like trees from long glasses. And now come the big dishes of new potatoes, flakes of skin barely hanging on. And Jack is back again with his jokes and a turkey cut up on a big blue plate. On a side table, two little dolls called Bridie and Joe sit on top of the wedding cake.

Jack picks up one of Mrs Nolan's knives and ticks a glass until silence falls. 'Now,' he says, face red to the roots of his hair, 'if you'll all just help yourselves.'

She walks across to the window and peeps through the curtain, wondering why Milly is so late. Beneath the window is Mrs Lennon's trolley – the sweet trolley, her sisters are calling it. Glass bowls puffed up with trifle. Tiny buns, sugared biscuits, dusty Turkish delights, and there's Mr Clifford's chocolates with the lid removed and already the best ones are missing. Mrs Nolan is beside her saying, 'Go on, take one.'

'Ah no, thanks, Mrs Nolan.'

'Ah, take one sure.'

'No, I'm grand.'

'Ah sure, why wouldn't you take one and the tongue hangin' outta your head?'

She reaches across and then thinks about Kay. 'No, I'll wait. It's all right.'

Mrs Nolan starts to insist. But then Milly walks into the room and the chocolates no longer matter.

'Oh, Milly! I thought you'd never get here.'

'My mother said I had to wait. Seeing as I wasn't really invited. As such.'

'Yes, you were.'

'Well, not to the whole thing then.'

Milly looks cross, so she says to her, 'Your yellow dress is only gorgeous, Milly. Do you like mine?' She positions herself for yet another twirl, but Milly goes, 'Mmmm,' and then walks away to peep through the adults and the table behind them. She comes back in a minute with, 'I see you have our blue china.'

'Have we? Oh, thanks for the loan.'

'Don't mention it. It's not our best set anyway,' Milly says, and then, before she has a chance to tell her the news about her glasses, walks off again and starts talking to Joe's nephew Billy.

Down in the kitchen, Mother fits dessert dishes into one another.

'Where's Eddie?' she asks.

'Oh, he wanted to walk back from the church – is he not here yet?'

Mother looks over at the clock on the wall.

'I see Granny Greene has arrived,' Eileen says, pushing past her.

'Her name is Millicent,' she answers back.

'Honest to God, what is wrong with that one? You should see her, Mother, stuffed into that frilly dress, the size of her.'

'She is not, Mother! She looks lovely.'

'She looks ridiculous. And swingin' out of Joe's nephew too – she's starting early I must say. The poor lad is only terrified.'

'You shut up, Eileen. She's my friend!'

She sulks out of the kitchen and stops at the scullery curtain. On the far side she can hear Maureen whispering to her best friend Belinda: 'Bridie put them under the sofa, you see. To keep them safe. And you'll never guess what that drunken blaggard did?'

'What? What?'

'Fell asleep on the sofa. And weed in his trousers. It dribbled down through the cushions. The chocolates were –'

'Oh my God! I don't believe you. Oh my God! That's just –'

'Destroyed.'

'And you had to throw them out?'

'We didn't dare. Not after Cliffy buying them. Of all the people … Eileen washed and dried them. They're upstairs on the sweet trolley. Just you make sure you don't eat any. And here – promise, now won't you promise, you won't?'

'As if!'

She walks back up the scullery stairs and her face is on fire. How could he? The chocolates. Mr Clifford's chocolates. Poor Mother …

Millicent is standing in the hall. 'This is so boring,' she says, 'they're all gettin' piddly-eyed in there. I'm sorry I ever came. The turkey's all gone. And I hate ham in anyway. When are they cuttin' the cake?'

'Not for ages.'

Milly tuts.

'Why don't you go in and have a few chocolates while you're waiting?'

'Chocolates?' Milly brightens up. 'Where?'

*

'Are you not goin' to give us an oul song?' Mrs Clingy-Clancy asks, squeezing her shoulders then rubbing her arm. She says to her husband, 'She's a great little one on the pian-o, I hope you know.'

'Oh, yeah, yeah, yeah. Righ',' Mr Clancy says.

'Terrific. Only terr-ific.'

'Oh, I don't think I could. Not in front of all –'

'Ah come on,' Mrs Clancy says, and starts fluffing up the skirt of her dress then gives her a little hug. 'Play something. What about "All for Marie's Wedding"? You do a lovely job on that. That's her special song. Marie. Get it?'

'Oh, yeah, yeah, yeah. Righ',' Mr Clancy says again.

Charlie walks in then and Mrs Clancy hooks onto his elbow.

'Tell her, Charlie. Tell her play "All for Marie's Wedding". Ah go on.'

'Yes,' he says, 'you should play it.'

'I have to help Mother, you see, and …'

'Well, after then. Say after the cake.'

'Oh, I don't know. I'd have to get my music …'

'Get it, sure we'll wait.'

*

No colour comes through the skylight, now that it's dark outside. She turns the door knob, slowly opens it, and the landing light makes a path for her to follow. At the bed she kneels and pokes her hand under the candlewick spread; the soft brush of it on her arm, the hard touch of her bag a little way in. She begins to slide it towards her.

There's the sound of a click then – not loud, just a click. And the shaft of light from the landing wobbles then disappears. For a second she can see nothing at all.

Everything moving so slowly it's almost as if it's not moving at all. Hands grab onto her back. She feels herself being lifted up, and at first she thinks it's one of her brothers trick-acting. But the hands are too rough with her, flinging her onto the mattress then flipping her over onto her back.

She makes out who it is then. There, at the end of that outstretched arm. She can see the loop of his silver watch chain. His large hands close in, pushing her small hands away and pulling at her good dress too, tearing its roses. She tries to scream, but her voice won't come out.

He is taking something out of his trousers now. And one pinstriped knee is up on the bed, now the other knee. His face grows larger and nearer, it keeps saying, Shhh, shhh now shhh. Even though she isn't saying a word and her screams are no more than a catch in her throat. She can smell little puffs of whiskey from his breath, and is so scared that she can't get her voice to make even a whisper. And now her hands have stopped working too. They just lie there dead by her side doing nothing. Why won't they move for her? Why won't they help?

Everything pitch black suddenly – the cloth of her dress is over her face, the sound of her petticoat crunching; it's like her dress is trying to drown her. She can't even hear the sound of her own breathing. She can hear his breaths, though, short, heavy, sharp. His voice goes, Shhh shhh now, keep quiet there's a good girl, good girl. Good girl.

Far away, there's another shushing sound. Shh shh, shh now. Silence everyone. Pray silence for the speaker. Shh! Shhh!

It's coming up the stairs from the parlour, and she can hear Charlie speaking thickly, the words he's been practising all week. She tries to call out to him, but everything is fading. She is going to faint. Just about to disappear when she feels one of his hands clamp onto the top of her leg and out of nowhere, and all on their own, her own hands come to life again and start flapping around like two little birds. They slap her dress back down, then curl themselves up, tighten into fists, fly up and PUNCH straight into his glasses, smashing the lens. He pulls back, puts his hands on his eyes, bends over and says, Jesus!

Her legs take her somehow over to the door; it swings open, the dressing-gown hits against her face as she flies through, bringing the sound back into her voice.

Downstairs they are singing; feet bangbanging on the parlour floor.

And there's Eddie in the alcove in the hall, sitting on the little seat beside the table, elbow resting on its corner. She wants to run down and tell him, to make her sobs open out into words. She wants him to bash Mr Clifford before he sneaks down the back stairs – already she can hear him gathering his things in the room above.

Eddie will get him. Eddie is the one. Charlie is too soft. Charlie is afraid of almost everything. She'd be too shy to tell Jack. Jack goes red if you ask him to pass the salt. Maureen might kill her – the price of Mr Clifford's glasses. And now the lodger's money gone too. What about Kay? Oh, look at her dress. Her lovely … And Mother. What would Mother say? What does Mother always say when you bring home complaints about the teacher from school?

'Eddie?' she calls down the last flight of stairs in a long, loud whisper. 'Eddie!'

109

Slowly, he looks at her. And yet he doesn't look at her. His elbow slips, his head drops down to his chest and it looks like he's fallen fast asleep. 'Eddie!'

Her feet start to move down the stairs. One step, then two … But the song from the parlour makes them stop. She listens:

'Step we gaily on we go,

Heel for heel and toe for toe.

Arm in arm and row on row …'

They are singing her song. Her special song. They said they would wait, but they started without her as if she just wasn't there. And it doesn't sound right either; it sounds all wrong.

She sits down on the stairs, holding on to the banister. It comes to her then. Yes, that's it. They've changed the words. Instead of 'All for Marie's Wedding', they are singing 'All for Bridie's'.

One word and now it's a different song.

Teatro La Fenice

We walk together, Claire and I, across the lawn that leads down to the edge of the river towards the smooth stone steps that will take us there. We pass Mr Fleming, who keeps the grass laundered, ironing green stripes, light and dark, with the big yellow machine that goes before him. Behind him the house is tall and russet red. There are forty-two windows in all, and most of them are the image of each other. Except for the window in the turret, which curves slightly towards the gable, and also the windows with the bars jammed into them, hidden in the bottom part of the house.

When we reach the steps we stop for a moment, Claire organising her hand in mine. Then slowly we take them one at a time, one foot leading, the other joining, and a little rest in between. Claire tells me this is because I am nervous and that I'm afraid I might fall on my face.

The grass is tougher here on the edge of the river, not so nice to the touch, and so Claire lays out a Foxford rug. She calls this 'our usual spot'. Guiding me down then to sit on one corner of the rug, moving my legs so that my knees face the centre, she then sits herself on the opposite corner in the same way, her knees facing mine. And that's how we are, Claire and I, two old biddies really. That's how you find us. Like a brace of old fairground ornaments on each end of a mantelpiece.

Claire's fingers begin to move, slowly clawing the back off an orange. When it's naked she hands it to me, and I hold it loosely on my palm. I wait for her to encourage me to eat, and, as I'm listening to the gnaw of my mouth on its flesh, Claire begins to speak.

'I suppose they were good enough to invite me. But at the same time, I'm not sure I feel like it – they've a nice garden though. Such a nice garden. And decking, if you don't mind.'

'Oh, decking – imagine that now?' I say.

'Yes. With a special place for cooking sausages in the corner. In the summer, like a barbecue, but, you know, much more sophisticated. It has a lid on it. Though by the time the sausages cook through, would it not be quicker to fry them on a proper pan? On a real cooker? Then bring them outside. Giving herself work, is what I say. It's a nice big garden all the same. Though, do you know, not a flower in it. And, I mean to say, what's a garden without flowers? I always insisted on looking after the flowers in our garden. No, Jack, I'd say, let the gardener see to the orchard and the lawn, but the flowers are mine. Jack used be livid.'

'Livid?'

'He liked me to look after my hands, you see.'

She stretches her fingers out and presses a plump mauvish hand into the sky.

'And there's my daughter-in-law with not a flower.'

'Not a flower?'

'Ah, daisies sometimes for a while. But she cuts them. You know, with an electric lawnmower.'

'Cuts them?'

'Yes, you have to plug it in.'

'In the garden?'

'Ah no. In the house. Then you have a big lead that you bring outside.'

'Now! Imagine that!'

Claire continues about the garden. She only stops to dab juice away from my chin or to pull a cardigan that is already there across my shoulders. She is always fussing, but it doesn't really bother me. And she doesn't demand much in return, except my company and the odd little word or question just to show that I'm minding her.

And you'd have to be minding what Clare says. That memory – where she keeps it all! Down to the finest detail. I only see things in a block, one picture at a time. What comes before or what happens after – well, I'm not always in charge of the sequence.

The river is twitchy today. The river has come all the way from the city – Claire once told me that. In the city it's big and wide and stinking to the high heavens. By the time it gets to us it has sweetened. And shrunk. Twitchy and wrinkly and grey.

On the far side of the river, some distance away, is a thick, tall wall made of random stone.

'That's the park over there,' Claire says, 'the Phoenix Park. That's where we're not allowed go, I hope you know that now.'

'Oh yes, Claire, I do know that now.'

'I thought maybe, by the way you were staring up at it, that you'd forgotten, like.'

'Ah no. Ah no, Claire, not at all.'

'Well, that's good,' she says and then she goes back to the garden, her garden or her daughter-in-law's, I can't be sure which.

There are times when I might like to say more. To contribute to one of Claire's conversations. But I'm afraid to risk it. How can I say, for instance, Yes, I was the same about my own garden, my own flowers? When I can't be quite sure if I had a garden at all, never mind flowers. And even if I was sure I ever had a garden, she'd be bound to trip me up. Bound to ask me name, rank and number of every last flower in the bed, and I'd never be able for that. Besides, she's happier with things as they are, her doing the talking, me doing the agreeing. I like her being happy too. We're great pals, Claire and I, great pals. Everyone says so.

'And do you know,' she continues, 'they don't even have a fry of a Sunday morning. And I do love a sausage and rasher of a Sunday morning, a nice bit of pudding too.'

'But I thought they had sausages on the boat?'

'Boat? What boat?'

'The deck-thing, you know. The thing that you said.'

'I said the decking. It's got nothing to do with a boat. It's attached to the house, for God's sake – will you ever listen?'

'Oh yes, that's right, of course. The house.'

Claire looks as if she might be going to sulk, but then she changes her mind. 'I could never face the golf course until I'd a decent feed: a rasher and egg and that – you know, like? That's the worst about going

continental, I always say. The breakfast. No fry. A bit of
old cake and a spoon of jam.'

'A spoon of jam.'

'Yes. And then there's Mass. I know full well they never
go except when I'm there. And, well, to tell you the truth
I'm not that keen any more. All those strangers trying to
shake your hand.'

'The Continentals?'

'Ah God, no. The church near where Gerard lives. Any
church, really, nowadays. That sign of peace business. A
way to pass germs is all that's good for. But they insist
on going just because I'm there. I'd just as soon walk in
the garden, talk to God in my own way there amongst the
flowers.'

'Except there aren't any.'

'What?'

'Flowers. There aren't any flowers.'

'Oh, yes, except for that.'

Now there, for example. I'd like to say something at this
point. Not about God, not about handshakes. Not so
much about the rashers or anything else in the fry either.
But, well, going continental. Claire is always talking about
what it's like going continental. And, for all I know, I might
know just as much about it as she does. I see this picture
of myself so often. Well, my hands really. Younger than
now, of course, but the same ring is on the same finger
and that's how I know it's me. And every time I look down
on this part of the river and every time I look over there
at the big old stone wall on the other side of the river,
I see it like it's on a screen. This big picture of a hand.

The hand (the one that belongs to me) is holding another hand (that doesn't) – a hand with wider fingers and a sprig of black hair just under the knuckles. A man's hand. No doubt about it. And I really love it, that other hand. I just feel this huge gulp of love for it. For a hand!

We are walking through streets so narrow that the hands have to split and my fingers creep up and crawl around his arm instead. We cross a bridge, a baby bridge, so small. And the sound of the water slapping and slurping and there's all these blobs of light crawling around on the stone like something under a microscope. Then we come out into a big square with tables and chairs and people and smells and it's all so … but how could I say that to Claire? How could I tell her that my hand is happy somewhere that might be foreign?

Oh, that would be lovely all right for her to take back to Matron.

'And supposing,' Claire says now, 'supposing the weather's bad? I'll be stuck indoors. Watching telly. They don't even go out of a Saturday afternoon. Would you believe it? She talks on the phone for about three hours. And he? I don't know what he does be doing with himself. He's gone as fat as you like too. And the kids eat rubbish and lie on the floor watching the telly with me and, like, I'd have to watch whatever they want. And I used to love going out of a Saturday. A bit of shopping and then a stop off at Thompsons or the Green Door maybe for tea. Oh yes, the Green Door was the place. Best hat and gloves for the Green Door. Nothing less would do, you know.'

She turns slowly and stares into my face. 'Besides,' she goes, 'what will you do? If I take up their offer. All

weekend. All on your own. Friday, Saturday and Sunday –
you know, it's a long old time.'

'Me? Oh, don't worry about me. I'll be as right as a
raindrop!'

I go back to my picture on the wall. The hands have locked
again. We cross the square to these steps on the other side.
A big flight of steps that grow bigger the nearer we get. We
climb. And then we're inside a marble hall, and all you can
hear are voices sort of purring, all the way up to the domed
ceiling. More stairs now, but different this time, red as lipstick and polished brown wood at the sides. My hand (the
one with the ring on) slides upwards and the man's hand
follows it. And then. Oh then, the magnificence of it all!
We come out into a place filled with rows of velvety seats.
And we sit down on one on the edge of a tier halfway to the
sky. Below us the hum and haw of an orchestra in preparation. Around us more voices talking and dresses crunching
and perfume and aftershave. Above us angels. Fat little baby
angels skirting a sky of blue and gold. And a thousand lights
winking in chandeliers. And I feel like – well, I feel like a cur-
rant in a wedding cake! A great big blue and gold wedding
cake. Imagine now, trying to say that to Claire?

Claire is so animated today. I know there'll be few moments
of peace. She's been on about this weekend for such a long
time. But of course that's the thing – I can't be sure how
long exactly. I seem to remember her speaking of it when
the river was low. And it's full today. I also feel I've heard
it when I was wearing my blue tweed coat and, yes, that
skirt which she is now tucking around my legs is cotton

red. Definitely red. Perhaps that was another weekend, one from a long time ago.

'You see the thing is,' she says, 'if I say yes then Gerard will have to drive all the way up from Cork to collect me. And he's so busy, 'twouldn't be fair. Though he has a beautiful car, I must say. Twenty-eight thousand it cost him. Twenty-eight.'

'Now. Imagine.'

'Sure, I don't think my own house cost that when we bought it.'

'It must be very big.'

'Oh yes, even the boot is –'

'No, your house.'

'Oh yes. My house.'

She says nothing now for a while. I can hear the river whisper and mumble all sorts of secrets. Mr Fleming's machine wheezes back to it. And it's all so very pleasant, this conversation of sounds with no voices.

'He has a phone too in his car,' she starts again, 'he speaks into it while he's driving along.'

'Ah, go away!'

'Oh, yes, they have several, you know. All over the house.'

'And in the car, did you say?'

'In the car. A real one. A real telephone.'

'Plugged in at the house?'

'Ah, not at all.'

'Well how then …?'

'Ah. You know. These things have their own way of working.'

Now what I think is this: if he has so many phones, why doesn't he ever ring Claire?

Even I get the odd phone call from – well, I don't quite know who. Not that I really want it, having to cross over to the phone with everyone grinning at me and making boyfriend jokes.

The next time whoever he is phones up, I know what I'll say. I'll say, 'Would you like to speak to Claire? Ah do. She loves an old chat.' Yes, that's what I'll do.

Claire stands up, and I know its time for her foot-dip. She says there's nothing like river water for chilblains and corns, but we must never tell anyone about her dip. In a moment she'll walk to the end of the bank to the little ornamental bridge put in by a very important man who used to live here a long time ago, before Matron and the nurses took over. He was the man who betrayed Charles Parnell, Claire said. She will climb down to the little ledge near the bridge and sit herself down and dip her feet in, water curling around her legs and cuffing her ankles. Sometimes you can hear her giggling down there.

But first she has to get herself ready. And off they come, rolling down in little creases and turning her legs from brown nylon poles to purple gnarled ones. She's let the pants slip down as well by accident and I thank God Mr Fleming can't see this far, her bare bottom, like two big pork chops hanging down. And I noticed that, too, her pants are soiled. Oh, only slightly, but enough to cause shame. And I could easily do it too. Tell, I mean. I could easily say, 'Claire is not wiping herself properly.' After all, who told on me when I had that little accident with the sheets?

She stands before me now, pulling her skirt down carefully over her knees. 'No,' she says, 'I've decided. I'm not going. No, no. That's it. I've made my mind up.'

'Your mind?'

'Yes. At the end of the day, I just couldn't have it on my conscience leaving you all alone all that time. Well, supposing something were to happen to you. Or if you had one of your little accidents. Who'd cover up for you then? Sure you'd be lost without me. Anyone will tell you that.'

'Anyone?'

'Well, everyone then.'

Everyone says I'd be lost without Claire. But I wouldn't be lost, how could I? There's nowhere to get lost except for the big park place across the river and I'd never be able to find my way there. Unless I swam across.

Why, even here in the house, I couldn't get myself lost. There are no more than three or four routes to be considered anyway, and there's always someone you can follow if you find yourself getting confused. Not once in all the time I've been here have I forgotten. Not once. Except for –. But that doesn't really count because that time I only pretended to be lost. Matron was so cross, I had to let her think it was an accident. The truth is I was just curious, that's all. That's why I followed her.

I wanted to see what was behind the door that needs the two keys. It's a green door too, but not Claire's green door in Cork city. And what was behind it? Not gloves or hats anyway. Not pots of silver tea either – but Purgatory. That's what.

The name came into my head the minute I set eyes on it. 'Purgatory!' I said it out loud and the matron heard and that's how she knew I was there. Nobody belonging to this world or the next. People inside all crying and moaning, all trying to rock themselves back to this life or on to the next one. And the smell! A smell of rabbits – that's what it was.

Claire says they're all in there on account of having eaten the aluminium off the bottom of the pans. Well, I ask you! They must have been mad in the first place – why else would they do such a thing? Luckily for Claire she never had aluminium in her house, only copper. Only copper would do.

Anyway that day, the day Matron found me, she dragged my arm back into the main room and I followed it. And as I sat back down in my place I made myself a promise: that I was never going to end up behind that door. And how was I going to do that? By keeping my mouth shut.

And was I glad to be back in our own main room? Our lovely own main room. They call it the Chinese Room because of the hand-painted designs on the wall. A very important man used to live in this house. Just him and his family – they had it all to themselves. He was the man who sold Parnell up the river. And you'd want to be very important to be able to do that.

A large room, the Chinese Room; each allotment of space is taken up by a chair, and on each chair a wispy grey head, like a jinny-joe, nods away the time between meals.

'What a beautiful room!' That's what the people from outside always say, looking around it, up and down, all through their visit, as though they'll be asked to recite every inch of it before being allowed go home.

And silence, always silence. Here only the radio speaks. Except for, of course, when the doctor comes.

Then it's a different matter. As soon as he walks through the door it starts. 'Doctor, Doctor, I've a sore this, a pain in me other, and not a bit well today Doctor, Doctor …' As he passes each one, the chorus reaches out and follows him. It's like he's Jesus walking among the lepers. When he leaves all is quiet again. Until the bells of the Angelus call out from a radio on top of the long-locked piano – then it's 'pish-pish-pish declared onto Mary' for a moment or two..

Claire used to have a piano in her house too – same colour, only much bigger.

Claire pulls her cardigan like a shawl over her head. She holds it tightly with the hands Jack liked her to look after.

'Gerard will be furious. And it's not as if I'm not disappointed myself. And the kids? Well, they love their old granny, you know.'

Then I remember something. 'That's right, Claire – your granny flat!' I say, delighted with myself. 'What about your granny flat? Surely you want to see that!'

Well. You'd think I was after doing something terrible. You'd think I was the world's worst.

'I thought I told you never to mention that to me? What sort are you mentioning that to me? What sort of a *bitch*!' She draws back her hand – it comes flying down and gives me such a punch in the arm that I topple over.

Claire walks away from me, huffing with rage, and I stay lying on my side on the ground.

And what did I say? What was it again – granny flat? But I thought she'd like to see the granny flat they built her. Wasn't that why she sold her own house in the first place, so that she could give them the money to buy a house with a big garden where they could build a flat for a granny?

Her funny long feet leave photos of themselves in the muck near the edge of the river. Soon she is there at the end of the bank. She tweaks the water with her toe, but she doesn't sit down on the ledge. She stays standing, her back to me, her face towards the distant wall of the Phoenix Park.

Can she see pictures up there too, I wonder. Does she see flowers, a house, a kitchen? Can she see Jack?

I would love to ask her. But I'm afraid her answer will be that the wall is only a wall. A big stone wall around a park we're not allowed into.

The House on Parkgate Street

I n school they called her Ghostie – a name she'd heard a few times before, popping out from a huddle of sniggers or in the echoes of the cloakroom toilets. By the time Gráinne made the connection she'd been in her new school for over a month and, coming out of a toilet cubicle one morning, had caught sight of herself in the mirror. Shaky and frail, even paler than usual.

There had been blood again and she hated all that: the appalling smell, the mess, the way you were supposed to wrap the pad up and put it into this bin that was already choking up to the neck with other girls' pads stained with other girls' blood. This was the third time of bleeding since she'd turned thirteen (she couldn't bear to use Mam's stupid word 'period') and the novelty had well worn off along with the little chats about womanhood and nature. Gráinne thought it was disgusting anyhow. And that she was disgusting too: hair sprigging up in all sorts of places and strange smells coming off her, no matter that she had a shower every day and in between powdered and squirted and sprayed. 'Taking a tart's bath' was what Mam called it when she did that.

As soon as she saw herself in the cloakroom mirror, the name 'Ghostie' made perfect sense. Not just because of the way she looked – face as white as a page of paper. But it was her movements too – the way she had just closed the door behind her with hardly a sound while the other girls, even the shy ones, would nearly wallop it off its hinges. And her habit of sidling up to a group at break time and standing there saying nothing, or walking alongside a row of hockey players on the way to the pitch, craning to hear what was being said up the line even though it had nothing to do with her. And at the bus stop, of course, grinning at someone just because they happened to be wearing the same uniform.

Now the toilets were deserted. Every other soul in the school shut into a classroom. The only sound the gurgle of cisterns and a distant rumble of a teacher's voice. Gráinne took in a breath of bleach-scented air and placed her bony hands on the ledge of the sink. Rows of mirrors before and behind her, fractions of the cloakroom coming through: a crowd of coats clinging to a wall, a row of hollow, hard sinks. The back of her black head staring in at her white paper face and her pale lips leaning in to whisper, 'Ghostie.'

Before starting in her new school, Mam gave her a bit of advice.

'You know the way you can be a bit of a yapper?' was what Mam said, 'well, you should knock that on the head for a start. Most of the girls will already know each other from primary school and you don't want them thinking you're pushy. Some of them might be a bit on the rough side too – rougher than you're used to anyhow. Now, I don't mean be unfriendly – God, no. Hang about, share your sweets, smile to show you're listening and that. And laugh at a joke – but not too much. Just go easy on the yapping. Can you try that for me?'

'Okay, Mam, yes. Yes, I can try that.'

After Mam said that about her being a yapper, she couldn't stop thinking about it. It was something she hadn't known about herself up till then. She wondered if maybe she'd taken after Dad. Dad was from Liverpool and she'd often heard Mam say that Liverpudlians could spend the whole day talking about nothing. Since Mam and Dad decided to go their separate ways, as Mam always put it, he seemed to yap even more. He started the minute he picked Gráinne up on Saturday morning and he was still at it when he brought her home that evening at six. When he wasn't yapping to her, he would yap to strangers. In the pub where they sometimes went for their lunch, or in the shop where he bought his pint of milk and his small sliced pan and his little tin of beans and his one banana. Or in the café where they went for a cup of tea to get in out of the cold, or even when it wasn't cold, in the park where they went to feed ducks. In the end, she decided to ask him: 'Dad, you know the way you never stop talking? Well, is that because you're from Liverpool?'

His face turned roaring red; she could tell by his eyes that his feelings were hurt. She tried to explain about Mam's advice for starting her new school, and then she told him about the way the other girls had been calling her Ghostie behind her back. But all Dad said was: 'We can't all be the strong, silent type.'

The next day was Sunday and Dad rang her up. Mam answered the phone and Gráinne moved near the door to listen. 'Well, I shouldn't allow it really, it's not your day,' Mam said.

And then, with her voice getting tighter: 'Oh, really now? Is that right now?'

And then a bit higher: 'You weren't so obliging yourself that time when I asked you to take her for –'

And then all the way up to a shriek: 'She's my daughter too! Oh, shut up, just shut up. All right, you can talk to her, but don't keep her long, she has homework to do – Gráinne!'

Gráinne waited for a few seconds before coming out to the hall, where Mam stood holding the receiver like a gun in her hand. 'Your father!' she snarled at Gráinne, as if somehow that was her fault.

Dad said, 'I won't keep you long, Grawzer, just wanted to say – well, I've been thinking about what you were telling me yesterday, you know, that business about you saying nothing in school and finding out about the other kids calling you Ghostie and that?'

'Yes, Dad?'

'Well, we can't go against our own natures, love. Try being yourself for a change. You take my advice and talk as much as you want.'

And Gráinne said: 'OK, Dad, yes. Yes, I can try that.'

In October Dad had to go back to England because there were no jobs left in Dublin, and Gráinne cried when he told her that. He said he'd come over to see her whenever he could, and if he didn't come he'd phone. But if there was one thing she could absolutely one hundred and ten per cent rely on, it was this: 'Every

Tuesday, come what may, your pocket-money envelope will arrive in the post.'

'I'm glad it will come on a Tuesday, Dad,' Gráinne said. 'Tuesday is my very worst day in the week: double geography and boring civics and then having to go to Aunty Judy's house after school and stay overnight just because Mam has to go to her stupid French class after work and then for a drink with her friend.'

And Dad said: 'Friend. And what friend would that be?'

*

Mam often said how nice it was for Gráinne to be able to spend time with Judy. She said it like it was some sort of treat. And one time, when Gráinne said, 'I don't spend time with her – all I do is clean her dirty house,' Mam called her a cheeky bitch. 'Poor Judy, all on her own apart from little Decky and the responsibility of that oul bag on top of everything else.'

Judy was a widow. The oul bag was her dead husband's mother who just so happened to own the house, as Mam said when Gráinne asked why Judy didn't just send her home if she was that much trouble. Decky was nine years old and, no matter what Mam might like to think or say, he wasn't much company, always sniffing or picking his nose or with his hand down the front of his pyjamas when he was watching the telly. And in the mornings he mopped up his cornflakes with a thick slice of bread and butter as if it were soup, and that always made Gráinne feel sick.

Aunt Judy sometimes worked as a night nurse. In her uniform she looked lovely and crispy and clean. Otherwise, her hair was all tossy and there were nearly always stains on her jumper. In fact, she looked slovenly. Gráinne knew this was the word for Judy because she heard Mam saying it on the phone once: 'Well, poor Judy – God help her – can be a bit on the slovenly side.'

Gráinne had quite liked the word and put it into an essay. The teacher said, 'That's an interesting word, Gráinne. Well done.'

Gráinne had been all delighted until the word 'swot' hissed out from the back of the room, followed by a tongue making slurpy nosies and a voice going 'lick, lick, lick'.

*

'The thing about Judy,' Gráinne began, taking Dad's advice by talking to two girls from her year at the bus stop, 'I quite like her, I do – really. But since her husband died, well, she's just slovenly. That's all. And after he died she had to move in with his mother who's really creepy plus a while ago she had a stroke so she looks like this –'

Gráinne stopped to make the stroke face, and the bigger of the girls goggled her eyes and barked out a laugh.

'And I can't stand my cousin Decky either, always sniffing at everything like a little dog –' she paused to do sniffy Decky, but this time there was no laugh, and so she stopped doing it and continued to talk – 'I just hate it over there. The house is mad spooky and talk about manky! Anyway, that's where I go on Tuesdays and that's why I'm at this bus stop over here instead of the usual one over there, because I'm not going to my own house, see? I'm going to Judy's, which is in the same direction as you two. And so we'll all be on the same bus. Oh! And I just want to say, I only know the word slovenly not because I'm a swot or a lick or anything but because I heard and well …'

The two girls just stared at her. And the more they stared, the more she couldn't stop talking. She didn't even know their names because they always sat in the back of the class and only ever spoke to each other. One of the girls wore glasses and was gawky-looking anyway, her mouth always open and talking slow through her nose. Gráinne knew if Mam ever met her she'd say she was a bit on the common side. The other one was a big lump and her hair was greasy; so was the front of her uniform. She was stuffing her face with crisps that she hadn't even offered to share. She was, in fact, even more slovenly than Judy.

'Anyway, I'm going into the shop,' Gráinne heard herself say then. 'I'm just dying for a cone,' she added, because a cone in November seemed like an interesting thing to be dying for.

'Anyone else? I'll pay, I don't mind, Tuesday is my pocket-money day, see? It comes in the post from my dad with the money changed and everything. My dad is English, you see.'

The big one said, 'Englishhh? Is he?'

But the gawky one said, 'Big bleedin' trill.' Like she thought Gráinne was showing off about having an English dad.

But then the big one said, 'Here, I'll have a cone.'

And the gawky one shrugged. 'Go on, then. Get's one as well.'

She came out of the shop and the two girls were gone, and all around the bus stop was deserted except for a scrunched-up crisp bag on the ground. A bus was push-ing into the distance. Gráinne stood still. She kept hoping it might be some sort of a joke, that any minute now the two girls would jump out from a doorway or pop up from behind a parked car, and even a short while later, when the next bus came along, that somehow they might be on it, watching out for her and waiting on their ice-creams, laughing their heads off at the great joke they had played on her.

She should have thrown the cones, or at least two of the cones, into the bus-stop bin. Instead of walking down the aisle of the bus holding them like a bunch of flowers in her hands. Everyone staring at her and thinking she was a greedy bitch, eating three cones all to herself. Halfway down she found an empty seat. Gráinne sat in it, elbows held high. Her hands were full so she couldn't take her schoolbag off her back and had to stay perched on the edge of the seat. In the blurred reflection of the glass, she saw herself as a hunchback.

Even before she sat down, the ice-cream was melting, the trickles of red syrup blurring into the white. She took a lick off one cone, then the other, then the next. But no matter how fast her tongue moved, it couldn't keep up; dribbles all down the sides of the cones, over her hands and now creeping towards her wrists. A few seats behind her two boys were in fits laughing and a bald man in a green coat kept turning his head, pretending to look out the back window but really it was to stare at her. She could hear the conductor upstairs. Soon he'd be standing beside her.

Gráinne thought she might be going to cry. She could feel the fat pulse of a sob in her throat. She squeezed her eyes tight, but still one or two tears managed to escape. Then she felt someone tip her on the arm and a woman's voice say, 'Are you OK there, love?'

She turned her head just enough to see a woman leaning across the aisle from the seat opposite. But she was too ashamed to really look at the woman's face. 'They weren't all supposed to be for me,' she explained, 'see, I bought them for these two girls in my year and they said they wanted them, but a bus must have come along when I was in the shop because when I came back out they weren't – they weren't – well, they just sneaked off on me.'

'Ah, don't mind them,' the woman said, her voice hoarse, like she had a bad cold. 'Aren't they a right pair of wagons, now, to do that on you? Here, show us one.'

She reached across the aisle and plucked a cone from Gráinne's hand. Then she sat back into her seat and looked out the window. Gráinne thought the woman was going to eat the cone, but instead she lowered her hand and dropped it on the floor. The toe of the woman's white boot pushed it to one side then kicked it under the seat in front of her.

She looked over at Gráinne and nodded a few times, like she was telling her to do the same thing with the next cone. 'Go on,' she said, 'no one's mindin'. I'll keep watch.'

Gráinne let the second cone fall from her hand, then, just as she'd seen the woman do, drew it to the side with her foot before kicking it under the seat in front of her. She looked over at the woman. The woman laughed. Gráinne laughed back. Then the woman sat back into her seat and looked out her window.

Only one cone to worry about now. She began to turn her tongue over it, round and round. The bald man got off the bus and stopped to stare in the window at her before the bus moved off again. But all she could think of was Decky and Judy and her dead husband's mother who used to be called Mrs Connell before she had the stroke. And she remembered all the mean things she'd said about them and about their house to the right pair of wagons whose names she didn't even know. Her stomach felt cold and her tongue was numb and there was a sharp pain in the side of her nose. The bus turned for the bridge. The little park with the spiked railings came into view, and behind it, over the treetops, the name Ashling Hotel glowed red – this meant the next stop was hers. She dropped the remains of the cone on the floor and stamped on it.

The woman got off at the same stop and they waited together to cross over Parkgate Street. It was getting dark. In the headlights from the passing traffic, Gráinne took a good look at the woman. She wore loads of brown stuff all over her face, glittery purple and white on her eyes. But she didn't wear any lipstick, so her lips looked sort of baldy against all the rest of the makeup. Her skirt was short, a bit old-fashioned, Gráinne thought, and didn't really suit her anyway because her legs were a bit on the fat side. The boots reminded Gráinne of the ones Dick Whittington wore, only with a much higher heel. The woman's hair was lovely though: long and wavy and the colour of blackberry jam.

A motorbike twirled through a row of cars and passed right in front of them. The woman put her hand on Gráinne's arm and said, 'Mind!' Then she pulled Gráinne by the sleeve across the road as if they were going somewhere together.

'Which way are you going?' Gráinne asked when they got to the other side.

'The other way.' The woman nodded her head back towards town. 'I'm just going up here to get a few smokes first.'

'I'm going up here too – I'm staying with my aunt.'

A van beeped its horn and two men in overalls waved out and made faces at the woman.

'Do you know them?' Gráinne asked, but the woman didn't answer.

When they came to Aunt Judy's door, Gráinne stopped.

'This where the aunt lives then?' the woman asked, looking in the window of the empty shop beside Judy's door.

'Only since her husband died. That used to be his mother's shop. But she can't work in it now because she had a stroke.'

'I remember it right enough,' the woman said, opening her handbag and taking out then unwinding the cellophane from a new packet of cigarettes.

'You have cigarettes already,' Gráinne said.

'I know. But I need another pack. For later, like.'

'You must smoke an awful lot,' Gráinne said, and the woman laughed and said, 'You can sing that!'

'I help my aunt to clean up the house. I stay every Tuesday night and go to school from here on Wednesday. You wouldn't think it, but it's a huge house inside, four

135

storeys up and goes all the way down the back. Most of it is empty, but …' Grainne stopped then because she knew the woman wasn't really listening.

Gráinne looked at the reflection they made in the window of the empty shop. The woman lighting her cigarette in her short skirt and Gráinne almost as tall as her in her long gabardine coat. The floor in the shop was scattered with brown envelopes and coloured leaflets. The glass of the window was dusty, the sill inside pipped with dead flies. A sign in the window said 'For Sale or To Rent'.

The woman took a long drag then began to walk away.

'I like your eye make-up by the way,' Gráinne said. 'Did it take long to do?'

The woman laughed. 'You're a funny little one, aren't you?'

Gráinne shrugged.

'Well, better be off.'

'Are you going home now?'

'No. To work.'

'Well, thanks for helping me and, well, thanks.'

'You're welcome. Mind yourself.'

Gráinne called out after her: 'My name is Gráinne.'

The woman stopped and turned to look at her then blew out a frill of smoke from each nostril. 'Noreen.'

'Bye, Noreen.'

'Yeah, bye.'

*

Then it was Christmas. Dad saw her for a while on Christmas Day, but had to go back to England on Stephen's

Day, or Boxing Day as he called it. He gave her money in a card and a long pink scarf with bobbles on the end of it and a glass ball with a reindeer inside that showed a snow-storm when you shook it.

'I know it's not the same as the old one,' Dad said, and Gráinne wished he hadn't because now she had to remember what the old one was like and how it got broken.

'It doesn't matter, it's lovely.'

'I did look everywhere – all over Liverpool in fact – for one with angels inside.'

'It's OK, Dad, honestly.'

'Anyway, it was the best I could do.

Gráinne felt the weight of the glass ball in her hand. In her mind she could see the old one that her English granny had given her when she was five and that she'd kept safe all those years, only taking it out of its box every Christmas. There had been little angels inside, maybe three or four, she couldn't remember now, only that they were white and gold and delicate as insects. For a second Gráinne could see the sitting-room where they all used to live together, with the tree leaning into one corner and the television in the other corner and broken bits all over the floor.

'I love this one, Dad. In fact, I much prefer it.'

On New Year's Day he phoned her. 'This will be your year,' he said.

'How do you mean my year?'

'I mean, good things will happen to you.'

'How do you know?'

'Just a feeling. For a start, you'll be fourteen and I'll have to give you a rise in pocket money. And I bet every

Saturday when I phone you'll have something brilliant to tell me, something that happened to you during the week.'

When she put down the phone, she told Mam. 'Dad said this will be my year, and that every single week something brilliant is going to happen to me.'

'All talk, talk, talk,' Mam said, 'always the bloody same. Did you tell him you need a new coat?'

'No, Mam, I didn't. I mean, I didn't know I did.'

'Ha!' Mam said.

A few days later it was back-to-school Tuesday. The pocket-money envelope arrived as usual, and as usual Gráinne cut out the stamp and put it into a box even though it looked the exact same as all the other stamps in there. Then she put the envelope into her pocket to carry around for a few days and take out now and then to look at Dad's slanty writing. When next Tuesday came, she would carry the new envelope around and throw this one into the drawer where most of the pocket money ended up because, since she stopped going to the sweet shop after school, she couldn't think of anything to buy.

*

She woke to the silence of snow and the Christmas-card glamour it put on the dingy view out Judy's bathroom window. Moments ago Judy had shouted up that there was no point in her going to school with traffic at a standstill all over town. 'I'll ring your Mam, get her to come collect you after work.' And Gráinne, after rolling her eyes and miming a snarl through the bathroom door, had sweetly replied: 'All right, Aunt Judy, I suppose …'

The snow, at least, was clean; the air fresh on her face, she stayed for a while hanging out the window and wondered about the house behind her. How could Judy have made this her home? With its damp rooms and endless dark stairs; the random streaks on its walls that looked like sweat marks; the rusty smears on the bath; the vacant shop downstairs that nobody wanted; and then, right up at the top of the house, the flat where the old woman had lived for a while before she got sick. Gráinne had only been up there once, but she remembered it as the spookiest part of the house: photographs of dead people everywhere, and the fumes from the gas fire clogging the air had made little difference to the cold draughts hissing through the rat-a-tat windows.

When Gráinne came down, Judy was feeding the old woman from a bowl. 'It's all right, Gráinne,' Judy said. 'You don't have to be afraid of her. She's still the same woman, you know.'

'I'm not afraid, Judy! I'm not afraid of you, Mrs Connell, honest. I'm not!'

The old woman glared from her good eye. There was a worm of oatmeal on the corner of her mouth and her dead hand was plonked on the arm of the chair, a knot of skin and bones and veins. Gráinne looked away. The truth was she had always been a little afraid of Mrs Connell, even before the stroke had taken the best of her.

She studied the long kitchen table, piles of clothes waiting to be ironed at one end. At the far end, Decky, still in pyjamas, driving his dinky cars over the obstacle course he'd made from the dirty breakfast dishes. Engine sounds coming out of him: *erm erm beep beep.*

Gráinne began folding the clothes. It was still like a giant ashtray in here even though the old woman no longer smoked: a dirty, dry smell and burn marks on the furniture. Yet the kitchen had been a tidier place when Mrs Connell was in charge. She had always kept busy, minding Decky and cleaning the place or popping in and out of her shop. And always a cigarette perched nearby: on the side of the table, an ashtray, her bottom lip. Now she just sat in her special chair with the little desk-top fitted over one arm, pad and pencil by her good hand in case she wanted to write out a message. Gráinne thought of the way Mam had described Mrs Connell: 'Sitting there all day, in front of the telly, wearing her face like a mask that's on crooked.' Gráinne liked the clever way Mam sometimes described things. She remembered the sound of her voice when she had said that, the pity in her eyes. And she missed Mam then and wished she could just go home.

By mid-morning the sun was out and the snow on the ground was fading over the lumps of Judy's backyard. Gráinne cleaned the bath then buffed up the taps then piled all the dirty towels out to the landing. She came down and wrestled the hoover out from under the stairs. But when she plugged it in, it refused to lift anything and just sat there like a big fat pig, whining. She unblocked the hose then opened up the belly of the hoover. The bag was full. For a moment Gráinne considered calling out to Aunt Judy to ask where she kept the new hoover bags, but the phone started ringing then and anyway she already knew what the answer would be. Gráinne stuck her fingers into the dry grey guts of the hoover and tore out as much as she could, then wrapped the tangle of dirt into a newspaper and took it out through the backyard to the bin by the door that led into the laneway. She came back in, vacuumed the hall, then the upstairs sitting-room, then Aunt Judy's bedroom, then all the stairs. She vacuumed until her arm ached and the hoover started whining again.

When she came down, Judy was hanging up the phone in the lobby outside the kitchen. 'That thing hasn't stopped going all morning,' she said.

'I cleaned the bathroom for you,' Gráinne said, following her aunt into the kitchen. 'Oh, and the snow is melting now.'

'Ah thanks, you're a pet. What would I do without you?'

'I don't know. The traffic seems to be moving along fine too.'

'Thank God for that. I have to work tonight.'

'Oh yes, well, I only said about the snow because I've loads of homework and the books I need are at home and so I might just go now and not wait for Mam to collect –'

'Actually, Gráinne, I was going to ask you a favour. You know I said I've to work tonight?'

'Yes?'

'Well, Betty – she's one of my babysitters?'

'Yes, I know.'

'Well, her mother phoned earlier and, would you believe, she slipped on the ice last night and hurt her back.'

'What about the other babysitter?'

'She has the flu – or so she says.'

'Oh.' Gráinne looked at the floor.

'You know I wouldn't ask you, love, but there's no one else.'

'Wouldn't ask me what?' Gráinne said, but already she could feel her heart shrinking.

'I need someone to look after Decky and keep an eye on Mrs Connell.'

'Mrs Connell?'

'Gráinne, please, she's easily managed really. I'll feed her before I go and get her ready for bed so all you'll have to do is help her go to the toilet just before bedtime. And I'll give you a few bob for yourself – a good few bob. How about that?'

'But I have loads of money.'

'Well, I couldn't expect you to do it for nothing, now, could I?'

'I thought you said Mam was coming to collect me?'

'No. She phoned and said it's all right if you stay another night.'

'Mam phoned?'

'Yes.'

'But why didn't you –?'

'I did, but the hoover was on and you couldn't hear me. Anyway she said she'll ring you later.'

'But I've no clean pants, Jude, and I only have my uniform.'

'That doesn't matter. I'll give you a clean pair of pants.'

'I wouldn't like wearing –'

'Well, can't you rinse out a pair of your own pants? And I won't be on duty all night. Only until two – max.

Tell you what, you can call your mam if you like for a little chat – after we have lunch.'

Gráinne looked at the clock. It was half-past twelve.

'What time will we be having lunch?' she asked.

'Soon.'

*

At three o' clock Judy sent her out to the chipper. 'We may as well call it dinner now,' Judy said, and told her to get the works: three singles of chips, two long ray, a spice-burger for Decky and a large single for Mrs Connell because, with her slack jaw, that was about all she could manage. Gráinne set the table, buttered the bread and put the kettle on before she went because the last time, when Aunt Judy said she'd take care of it, she forgot, and by the time everything was ready the food had gone cold.

On Parkgate Street the wheels of the cars and buses squelched by. The sun had weakened most of the snow; only a few patches were left on the ground or blobs on the gutters and windowsills. Gráinne missed Mam again. She wondered how much trouble she'd get into if she just jumped on a bus and went home this minute. She could phone Judy as soon as she got there, make up an excuse on the way. But no excuse in the world – bar getting knocked down by a bus or going mental – would cover that kind of carry on. If she only could speak to Mam, tell her how scared she was about being in the house on her own with Mrs Connell. Mam might come over after work and help her to babysit – why not? She could always ask – beg her and beg her until she agreed. Gráinne glanced down the road to the phone box.

The girl on the switch put her straight through to Mam's boss, and Gráinne nearly died when she heard his voice. 'Sorry, my dear,' he said, 'Mummy's taking a late lunch. She's gone to do some shopping for her dinner party tonight. Like me to leave a little message for her?'

*

The chipper bag was warm and plump in her arms as if she were carrying something alive – a cat or maybe a baby – under her gabardine coat. Gráinne could feel the vinegary heat reach through her nostrils and wind all the way down into her stomach. She never ate much in Aunt Judy's house and was so hungry now that for a moment she forgot all her problems and could only think of getting back to the kitchen to line the chips along the soft white bread, watch them melt into the butter, squash another slice of bread on top then get stuck in. She was almost at the door when something caught her eye, something way down the road where Parkgate Street blended into Benburb Street.

Gráinne stepped off the path. That end of the street was in shadow, snow still sturdy on the ground. There were pub signs and B&B signs sticking out from red-brick walls. Two soldiers in dark-green overcoats were walking up from the direction of the barracks, berets bobbing along. A good distance behind them something was moving, almost mechanical; something white. The soldiers came to a big silver lamp post on a corner and slipped into the pub beside it, leaving a clear view behind them. Gráinne waited. White. Yes, white. White boots. White boots walking. The woman with the white boots. The woman called Noreen.

Gráinne felt an urge to talk to her. To rush down the road to her and tell her all about Aunt Judy's house and the creepy old woman and Decky still in his pyjamas and, more than anything else, about not wanting to babysit and missing Mam and wondering why she hadn't said anything about a dinner party and what did that mean, anyway, dinner party?

The further she got into the narrowing street, the more she began to feel afraid. It was so quiet down here, so cold out of the sun. No one around except for Noreen coming from the opposite end of the street, which was much longer than Gráinne had first realised. There wasn't even any traffic on the road, except for a green truck parked opposite the pub on the corner where the soldiers had gone. She passed the hotel and the back railings of the little park. She passed the B&B and came near to the corner. The ground was slippy. Her feet gave a short skid, then a long one – if she wasn't careful, she could drop all the chips. She decided it might be better to wait at the corner for Noreen.

Across the road the truck had wads of snow stuck to its roof, and over the top frames of the front windows, and more snow in two thick, slanted slabs across the front of the cab, so that it looked as if it had a big whiskery face. It had no load on its back and that made it seem as if it might topple over. There were cute little doll-house curtains hanging on the window.

Gráinne looked back down the road. She could see Noreen clearly now, coming out of the distance. Soon she'd have passed the barracks wall. She was smoking and staring down at the ground. She wore a long white scarf wrapped around her neck, and Gráinne could see the tails of the scarf fluttering behind as she walked along.

A rapping sound came from the truck, and when Gráinne looked over a man with a dark chin was looking out through the open curtains. He smiled at Gráinne and she smiled and nodded hello. The man was miming something through the window but she couldn't make it out.

She looked back up the road. Noreen was so close now that Gráinne could see the red of the woolly socks, which were sticking out over the top of her boots, and the scarf pulled up over her face like a mask.

The rapping sound again. This time Noreen must have heard it. Her head came up: she looked over at the truck then back over at Gráinne. She started to walk much faster, her feet making the odd slight slip. 'Careful, Noreen!' Gráinne called out to her. 'You'll fall if you're not!'

But Noreen didn't even look at her. She reached the corner and pulled Gráinne around it by the elbow. It was a rough pull, and Gráinne could feel Noreen's nails through the gabardine sleeve of her coat. She nearly dropped the chips with the fright.

'What the fuck are you doin' here?' Noreen said through her teeth, then pushed her into the doorway of the pub.

'I was just down the road and I saw you and –'

'Now you listen to me,' Noreen said, still holding her by the elbow and giving it a jolt now and then. 'You don't ever show your face here again, I'm tellin' you now. Or I'll break it for you – do you understand me? I'll fuckin' break it.'

Gráinne blinked; tears squirted up into her eyes. 'I'm sorry, Noreen, I am really. I didn't mean …'

Noreen let go of her elbow then pulled her scarf back up over her chin.

'You shouldn't be here. Go home. Go on now, I'm tellin' you. Get lost. And don't come back.'

Gráinne was crying now: 'I only wanted to say hello. I didn't mean – It's just that I was and –' She lifted the back of her hand to wipe the tears away from her face.

A silver car swished past, and Noreen's head turned to follow its sound. Gráinne saw then that the side of her face was bruised and that one of her eyes was black and swollen.

'Oh God, Noreen!' she said. 'What happened to your face? Did you have an accident?'

'Yes, that's right, an accident.'

'That's terrible. Oh no. Is it very sore?'

'Nah, it's not as bad as it looks. Listen, you better go home now. Go on, there's a good girl.'

'Sorry, Noreen. I didn't mean – I hope your eye gets – Anyway, I'll go now.'

'Ah, don't mind me,' Noreen said. 'I'm not in the best of twist today.'

She took a packet of cigarettes out of her pocket, handing a box of matches to Gráinne. 'Light that for us, me hands are stuck with the cold.'

When the cigarette was lighting, she said, 'Hold on till I get a few drags out of this and I'll walk you up a bit. And here, if that fella in the truck looks near you, ignore him – right?'

Gráinne looked at Noreen's eye again: black and yellow and slimy, it looked as if a slug was lying across it. Then she looked at Noreen's shaky hand, trying to hold on to the cigarette. 'Would you like a chip, Noreen?' she asked.

'I was wonderin' what the smell was,' Noreen said.

Gráinne lifted the flap of her coat away to show the big brown bag, then she opened it up and began coaxing a bag of chips out of the steaming pile.

Noreen laughed into the bag. 'Jaysus,' she said. 'Do you always have to buy everything in bulk?'

*

The face on Judy when she got back. Gráinne presumed it was on account of the lukewarm chips or the length of time it took for them to get there. Judy took the chipper bag off Gráinne, put it on the table and tore it up the middle; by now the paper was so soggy it just fell apart. 'I thought I told you get three singles and a large one?' she snapped, looking down at the two little bags huddled behind the long ray. 'And there's only one fish here, Gráinne.'

'I wasn't really that hungry –' Gráinne began, pressing her lips together in case they showed the lipstick of grease from the chips she had started to eat and then couldn't stop eating with Noreen in the pub doorway.

Judy poured out the tea. 'You know, Gráinne,' she said then, 'if you want to phone your mammy you only have to ask.'

'Oh,' Gráinne said.

'You don't have to go behind my back, you know.'

'Oh right.'

'I told on you,' Decky proudly announced, climbing up on the chair and squinting at the food on the table. 'I seen you out the top window, and you were coming out of the phone box.'

'I'm sorry, Judy,' Gráinne said. 'I just wanted to –'

'Doesn't matter. Your mam phoned me anyway. Look, I don't want to be giving out to you or anything but, well, all I'm saying is ask me in future – OK?'

'Yes. Yes, I will. Definitely.'

Decky started whining that his chips were cold and that one half of his spice-burger was missing, and Gráinne thought she was really in for it now. But all Aunt Judy said was, 'Ah, would you ever shut up with your moaning, Decky, for Christ's sake.'

Then she came back to Gráinne. 'Apart from anything else, what must your mam think? What must her boss think, come to that? I'll tell you what – that I'm too bloody mean to let you use the phone in my house. Probably.'

Judy dropped a pile of chips into Mrs Connell's bowl and began feeding them to her one by one, her hand returning to the table now and then to take a sup from her tea. Gráinne could see Mrs Connell's face appear and disappear over the crook of Judy's arm, her mouth sucking on another cold chip and one furious staring eye staring out.

*

At six o'clock Judy was all neat and smooth in her navy-blue coat and her spotty scarf and her hair pinned into its nurse's bun. 'I'm off now,' she said, and Gráinne felt her guts flop over.

'Now, I've left a few goodies in the press for you. And there's beans and toast there for your supper, if you want. Now, let me see – yes. Mrs Connell has been seen to. Decky is ready for bed.'

And Gráinne would have loved to say that Decky had been ready for bed since he got up that morning.

Judy picked up her bag and scrunched her keys in her hand. 'Look, if you like, you could phone your mam – say in about an hour? Give her a chance to get home from work and that.'

'Thanks, Aunt Judy, but it's all right.'

'What do you mean it's all right?'

'I mean I don't want to phone her.'

Decky asked her if he could stay up late and Gráinne said yes, in fact he could sleep all night on the sofa if he liked. Because even though she hated him, she was too scared to let him go to bed and leave her alone with Mrs Connell. She was flicking through one of Judy's magazines when Decky said, 'She's writin' sumpin'.'

'Who is?' Gráinne asked, as if she hadn't already noticed Mrs Connell lurched to one side, her good hand struggling across the writing paper.

Decky sighed and went over to his grandmother. Then he came back to Gráinne with a sheet of paper. 'Special delivery,' he smirked, 'for you.'

'Shut up you, Sniffy,' she said. 'You're not funny.'

'I'm tellin' on you,' Decky whined. 'You're not supposed to call me Sniffy, it's not my fault I have a – I have a whatyecallit ting in me nose.'

Gráinne snatched the paper off him. 'Tell all you like, you little rat.'

She looked down at the shaky scrawl of Mrs Connell's message – four small words that took up the whole page: 'I'd love a fag.'

'I'm sorry but you can't, Mrs Connell,' Gráinne said primly. 'You're not allowed to. Anyway, there's none. Judy doesn't smoke.'

A few minutes later Decky was back with another page: 'Up in the flat. On mantelpiece.'

'I can't,' Gráinne said. 'No way. Tell her, Decky, I just can't – and that's all about it.'

'Tell her yourself,' Decky sniffed.

At nine o'clock Decky's eyes started to droop in front of the telly, and Gráinne gave him a Mars bar and a puck in the ribs. Then the phone rang.

Mam's voice all bright and breezy.

'Hi, love – just ringing to check you're all right!'

'Yes, thank you.'

'Is everything ...?'

'Hope you're enjoying your party, Mam.'

'What party?'

'Don't bother lying – your boss told me you're having a dinner party.'

'I'm not having a dinner party. It's just one friend coming over.'

'Friend? And what friend would that be?'

Mam left a silence on the telephone.

'It's another man – isn't it? I knew it was. I just knew it. How could you – to Dad?'

'Don't be ridiculous, Gráinne. Look, we'll talk about this tomorrow.'

'Mam?'

'What?'

'Mammy?'

'What, love?'

'Do you know something – I hate you, I do. Leaving me with Decky and that creepy old woman, you know well she gives me the willies. Every time I look at her, I feel like getting sick. Well, I just hate you, that's all. Dad would never make me do something like this. Never. You could have easily come over and babysat if you weren't with your stupid boyfriend. Well, you can have him all to yourself now because I'm going to live with my dad!'

'Oh, Gráinne, grow up. Your dad can hardly take care of himself, never mind you. Don't make me laugh! As if he'd even want you.'

Gráinne slammed down the phone and began to cry.

When she came back in, Decky was conked out on the sofa, arms flung over his head, a rim of chocolate round his wide-opened gob. Mrs Connell's face was all flushed. Her good eye glittered. It stayed on Gráinne for a moment and then turned away. Gráinne knew then that she'd heard every bit of the row with Mam on the phone.

'I'm sorry, Mrs Connell,' she said. 'I didn't mean …'

But the old woman kept her face turned away.

'Look – tell you what, I'll go up and get you a cigarette.'

She opened the door of the flat to a long, narrow room and a yellowish mist from the streetlamps outside. Gráinne pressed the light switch, pressed it again, was not surprised to find the bulb was wasted. In any case, she could see well enough: the frames of the pictures on the wall with all the shadowy faces inside, like people looking out night-time windows, and on the shelf above the gas fire an uneven troop of knick-knacks all the way down to the end where, perched at a slant, was a carton of cigarettes. Gráinne lifted the lid: one pack remaining.

Downstairs again, she settled a cigarette into the twist of Mrs Connell's mouth, then struck a match and rubbed the flame against the tip. Mrs Connell's lips frantically tried, and failed, to keep a grip on it. Finally Gráinne had to wipe the spit off the tip then return it to her lips, holding it steady while at the same time tilting the slack jaw up to meet it. The old woman managed to suck the cigarette to life, and a small, soft veil of smoke broke over her face. But then she exploded: splurts and gasps and razor-sharp coughs. For an awful minute Gráinne thought Mrs Connell was going to choke. She moved to throw the cigarette in the fire so she could bang Mrs Connell on the back, maybe get her a glass of water. But her good hand came out and pounced on Gráinne's arm. Wait, her eye seemed to say. Wait.

They started again. After a while they fell into a rhythm: Gráinne holding the cigarette and tilting the jaw, Mrs Connell pulling, Gráinne withdrawing for a few seconds while the old woman turned the smoke over in her mouth and released it again. Halfway through, Gráinne leaned in: 'All right there, Mrs Connell?'

Mrs Connell nodded, a glint of greedy pleasure in her eye.

Later, when Decky was covered with a blanket, and Mrs Connell tucked up in bed, and the kitchen all tidied and the milk bottles out, Gráinne took the packet of cigarettes back upstairs and returned it to the carton. It had started to snow again, a slow, lacy fall, barely visible. Gráinne went over to the windows and sat on the ledge.

It was a view she hadn't seen before from this house, and it took her a moment to understand it. She was looking down on the roof of the building next door and, after that, the squares and triangles of the neighbouring rooftops. Further out, away from the buildings, was the patch of road facing the corner where she had eaten the chips with Noreen. She couldn't see the pub doorway from here, but she had a clear view of the silver streetlamp on the corner and, across from it, the spot where the truck had been parked, vacant now.

Gráinne stood and leaned into the window. An elbow had come into view under the streetlight. Another elbow. Then a knee. A shoulder belonging to somebody else. A different leg took a backward step. A whole woman then appeared. Followed by another woman. Finally the blackberry-coloured head of Noreen barged into the beam of light.

Bit by bit, fractions of woman came together to form a group. Women talking and smoking together, close to the corner. It dawned on Gráinne then that if she were to go down through the backyard and out to the laneway she could be there in a jiffy. It would be such a clever shortcut to Noreen. But Gráinne remembered then the promise she had made, and so it didn't matter how clever it was, it was stupid because it was no use to her.

The snow was thickening now, spinning out of the darkness. The women had started walking around to keep themselves warm. One by one, they came from the corner and stepped out onto the road, circling in and out of her view. She could see them flapping their arms and banging their hands together. A car slowed up and pulled in beside them; one of the women broke from the circle and went over to it. Gráinne could see her lean in the window as if she were giving the driver directions.

She looked up at the sky, into the spin of the snow: faster and faster it was coming. She couldn't stop looking. She thought of Mam and her friend and wondered if they were looking at the snow now. On the doorstep of their house or maybe from Mam's bedroom window. Then she thought of Dad and wondered if there was snow in Liverpool and, if so, if he was watching it, and from what sort of a window, and if he was on his own or if someone was there with him to yap to about the snow. And she thought of the truck driver too, maybe stranded on a country road, peeping out through his doll-house curtains.

She continued to watch the women turning and returning in the haze of streetlight. Her eyes were beginning to hurt, as if they were too heavy for their sockets, the snow making her dizzy and feel a bit sick. She knew she should probably go back downstairs and get into bed before Judy came home.

The Yellow Handbag

Under the trees at the edge of the crescent, Ashok waits in the car – a Mercedes E-Class saloon. He is parked in his usual place but not in his usual car and, like a poor man who has borrowed an expensive suit, he can't seem to get comfortable in it.

He has been here some time, perhaps as long as an hour and ten minutes. (He did check the dash-clock as he pulled to the kerb, but no longer recalls what it showed then). It is now eight twenty-two and, bumper to bumper, before and behind, the row is complete.

Twelve-and-a-half minutes to go.

Every day it becomes more difficult to get the timing right, what with the cheapskates driving in from the outskirts and parking up for the day. Moments ago he watched the last one get out of her car, take a sly look around before zapping it shut and trotting off to the tram stop on the far side of the green for the short glide into town.

She was wearing shoes held high by heels that looked like surgical instruments; a movie-style coat gripped her at the waist. An attaché case bashed off her thigh as she hurried along. He had felt certain that she must have been in some discomfort, perhaps even pain. Yet she could hardly keep from her face the grin of free parking.

Ashok remembers a time when such people wouldn't dream of leaving their nice shiny cars in this estate. Not for five minutes, never mind a full working day. He worries that the residents will begin to complain and that one morning he will arrive to see double yellow lines or, worse, one of those signs that says 'Residents' Permit Only'. And he is no longer a resident here – he is no longer a resident anywhere.

His car is his home. Like a snail he moves with it. Not, of course, this Mercedes E-Class saloon, which is just for today's cushy number. But his own more modest, yet no less appreciated, Ford Mondeo two-litre TDCi.

It is not the worst arrangement for a neat fold-up sort of fellow such as he, brought up to live in tight spaces. And it has the advantage of being wholly private, unlike the bustee in Bombay, which was anything but, and where a game of street cricket was often the only occasion when a chap got to really stretch out his legs. It's a simple matter of maintaining shipshape order – everything to its purpose and place. Ashok takes pride in his organisational abilities: he is a man very much in control of his life.

The boot of his car serves as his wardrobe – clothes folded into airtight packages; a rolled-up sleeping-bag kept to one side and a blow-up pillow that, in flattening down to the size of a fist every morning, manages to vaguely surprise him each time. The interior of the car, his main living area, is arranged as follows: toiletries in a zippy bag tucked into the cubby hole and a series of Tupperware boxes stacked under the front seats, the largest of which is marked 'Snacks etc.' – (bag of marshmallows, another of suck-sweets and cheese slices in cellophane) – chosen not so much for taste as for low crumbability factor.

A second box marked 'First-aid & Meds' is a trove of many remedies: some for ailments that may or may not return – a cold sore last April or a stye in the eye at the end of last summer. Others remain in constant demand, most particularly and in direct response to his recent lifestyle of convenience, Preparation H and a tin of bicarbonate of soda. Alongside this box, a pair of toilet rolls is neatly inserted courtesy of the lavatory in Buswell's Hotel, the provider of the plushest, also easiest to pilfer, toilet roll in town.

The box under the driver's seat, 'Admin-cum-leisure', holds all that is necessary for the smooth running of Ashok's life – passport, driver's licence and other documentation; for vocabulary improvement, a *Concise Oxford Dictionary* and a *Roget's Thesaurus*, the print in both cases being rather small (he keeps meaning, but forgetting, to buy a magnifying glass); and his old wallet – a good quality pigskin that was a gift from his mother when he was twenty-one, since replaced with the poor quality, though equally cherished, gift from his daughter, Sarla, last year, when he was forty-two. Here he keeps safe his gym membership card, less for bodybuilding purposes than for everyday showering, also discreet sock and occasional underpant washing. For pleasure and expansion of mind, there is his library card. At the side of this box is a torch for night reading, although whatever happens to be his library 'book of the moment' stays in the shelf under the steering wheel. This saves him having to rummage through Admin-cum-leisure every time he gets a lull in the day, which lately has become more often than not.

Most useful of all, perhaps, are Ashok's notebook and journal. The former is a record of many lists: locations and opening times of various cafés, takeaways and late-night launderettes and includes a margin for marks out of ten awarded or deducted in each case. There is a further section for business concerns: advance bookings, cancellations etc. And a few pages set aside, although as yet remaining blank, for ideas for personal or entrepreneurial development. A list of forthcoming events completes this section: sporting and entertainment, major or minor, but in any case likely to attract crowds and therefore conducive to business. Also the closing times for nightclubs, late-night cafés and other glorified brothels about town.

The journal – cover neatly inscribed 'Regarding Sarla' – is of a more personal nature, essentially a record of access to his daughter: dates and times, denied or allowed. Maintenance payments: honoured or, indeed, still owed. And a one-sentence summary of encounters with his estranged wife over the past few years. These vary greatly in mood but a random sample might typically be: 2 December 2008, 'I know by the light of longing in her eye that she wants me back in her bed.'

Or 25 December 2008: 'The bloody witch will not rest until I'm a limbless destitute, pissing and shitting on the side of the road.'

Finally, there is a small photo album for moments of loneliness. Although Ashok finds this can exacerbate rather than soothe such situations.

All in all there are many advantages to this compact lifestyle, the freedom to sleep wherever he likes being the main one.

His preference would be the Phoenix Park, which, despite occasional hairy moments, allows the most privacy, particularly when caught short during the night. Following one such moment of particular hairiness, when he was lucky enough to get away with his life, Ashok was forced, for a time, to explore the alternatives.

On a side street in Donnybrook, a woman in a flimsy nightie, curtain held high (comma of armpit hair clearly on view), had stared down at him from a top-floor, fully lit window and shamed him into moving on. In Hume Street, a policeman had taken his details. In the car park of an ugly suburban hotel, a Russian security man had racially abused him. Another time, when he'd slipped in behind the row of trucks near the Ashling Hotel, he found himself plagued by women banging on the window half the night, offering knock-up services at knock-down prices. Ashok had politely but firmly declined. He refused to pay for love. And besides, the women on offer had been most unattractive. To borrow the term from his former flatmates, they were, in fact, 'mingers'.

And so it was back to the Phoenix Park.

As there are advantages to this self-contained lifestyle, so too are there drawbacks. The foremost of which is having 'no satisfactory place of residence for Sarla's visits', to quote from his solicitor's letter of the 14th ult. A fact that went against him at the access hearing the month before last. He could not seem to get it into his solicitor's fat head how preferable a Ford Mondeo was to the stinking hole on the South Circular Road, which, up till that point, it had been his misfortune to share with three low-life, high-drinking, foul-mouthed reprobates. The air festered with the smell of cigarettes, alcohol and farts, the walls rankled with posters of bare-tittied women corner to corner. If he himself had been unable to endure any longer these living conditions, how on earth could he expect his twelve-year-old daughter to spend time in such an environment?

This was the question Ashok had put to his solicitor again and again, but which his solicitor, despite all his nodding and muttering of yes, yes, and yes, had ultimately failed to pass on to the judge.

Number two drawback is this: if his Ford Mondeo is his home, it is also the place of his everyday work, that is to say, taxicab. And as any self-employed person can tell you, running a business from home can present its own problems.

He thinks now of the priest he picked up at the airport yesterday in a drizzle of morning rain. The way he had rolled down the window as soon as his ample backside pressed itself into the back seat of the cab. Rain squirting in over the rim and left hand held over his nostrils and upper lip, like he was hearing confession. Ashok had to wonder if, despite his best efforts, his Mondeo was beginning to stink. He resolves to check later, in an objective manner, as soon as his nostrils have had a chance to experience life elsewhere and return refreshed to his homestead, at present parked and patiently waiting in a back alley in

Rialto, where he earlier exchanged it for this Mercedes E at the garage of 'Burke's THE De Luxe Chauffeuring For All Your Chauffeuring "Need's"'.

It was Burke himself, also a taxi man, with a sideline in the 'chauffeuring racket' and a fondness for punctuation, who kindly passed him this job. Burke has a face the colour and texture of naan dough, a fact that Ashok tries not to think about whenever they speak to each other. He refers to these jobs as 'cushy numbers'. The first time he offered to put one Ashok's way, he asked if he was familiar with the expression.

'Oh, yes, Mr Burke,' Ashok had replied, pleased for once to be able to contribute something useful to the conversation, 'in fact, it is a term that is derived from the Hindi word *khushi*, meaning something that brings pleasure with little or no effort. The spelling, of course, is quite different – that is to say k–'

But Burke had rudely cut off the spelling lesson. 'Yeah, yeah, whatever. But I'm talkin' about the real reason they call them cushy numbers. It's not because of the high rates and juicy tips, you know. It's because you spend so much time in the car waiting on the punter that you better have a good cushy under your arse.' Ashok had understood that he was expected to laugh. And so he did, as heartily as he could, while at the same time wagging his finger, as though to imply that Burke was quite the rogue. A reputation, Ashok suspects, Burke would dearly like to enjoy.

Cushy or *khushi*, Ashok likes these numbers for another reason – they allow enough time to get acquainted with the passenger and so enjoy a real conversation. This makes a change from the usual snatchy chats of the shorter fare about Dublin, where he is as likely to get a sneer as a tip. Or worse, a babble of drunken nonsense and an attempt, all too often sucessful, at dodging the fare. Riffy-raff types, as uncle Ravi used to say.

He picks the information sheet from the passenger seat and checks the details again: Flight DL102 arriving from JFK via Shannon at 10.25. Passenger Mr J. P. Ridell.

He has no idea what to expect from his passenger: age, appearance or even itinerary. Mr Ridell may want to be taken on a tour at once; he may want to go straight to his hotel. It will all depend on the jet-lag situation. Ashok knows only this: that he will be waiting at the barrier with his sign held high and his chauffeur hat at the correct angle, and that he will be available to the client's becking and calling for the rest of today into tonight, when Burke himself will take over. And that whatever else Mr J. P. Ridell will be, he will be a VIP.

A Very Important Person indeed.

Ashok's definition of a VIP is this: someone who knows not just how to receive respect, but also how to give it (the exception being VIPs from his own part of the world, in which case they will simply treat him like shit). A VIP is a gentleman who is inclined to conversation. Conversation that is both intelligent and meaningful. This is most particular to the longer drive when, after a few hours in a shared intimate space, tongues loosen and hearts relax, words are divulged that otherwise might have remained unspoken.

At the end of such days it is not unusual for Ashok to be able to say – either to himself or even occasionally to someone else (a counter hand in a chip shop or perhaps a fellow launderette customer) – 'Oh, yes, in my line of work I meet some very interesting people indeed.'

Ashok shifts around in the driver's seat, stretching his legs. He lays his hand on the burr walnut trim of the dashboard of what, he has to admit, is quite possibly the finest car he has ever had the privilege to drive. No need here for artificial aids such as air-freshener trees or flower-flavoured spray. In a car of this calibre, leather and wood provide their own sweetness. And although, as a rule, Ashok can't understand or condone the way some men speak of cars in a sexual manner (in his opinion a car is a car and no substitute for a woman), he would gladly admit that the Mercedes E-Class is a thoroughbred of automation. But if he had to, absolutely had to, call it a woman, then Aishwarya Rai, the Bollywood star, would be its name. But then again, in case nobody knew to whom he referred and therefore remained unclear as to the extent of his admiration, he would probably say Elizabeth Taylor in her hot-tin-roof days. Not much before then, and certainly no later.

He notices the smudge of his thumb-print on the walnut trim. Throwing a soft breath over it, he gives it a wipe with the sleeve of his jacket. Then glances at the dash-clock again. Eight more minutes to go.

He will see her. He tells himself that's all that matters. He may not, indeed should not, speak to her, but that is acceptable also. Seeing is believing. And should somebody ask him – as Burke did only this morning when he called to collect the Mercedes – 'So tell us, do you get to see your daughter at all these days?' he will be able to say in all truth, 'Oh, yes, indeed, I see her each day before school, without fail.'

He looks out the window. Across the green facing the crescent, a trio of school uniforms comes into sudden view. Soon the whole area will be swarming with the dark, dull colour of cabbage. Even after all his years here, Ashok still finds it strange to see so much of the one dreary colour being worn by so many teenage girls at one time. He is convinced that it drags them down, perhaps even contributes to their heaviness of step, the fact that their smiles are seldom or that they appear to be in a perpetual sulk. He thinks now of his own sisters and their friends at that age, delicate and impermanent as butterflies. Their lightness of step and laughter. Despite everything.

Six minutes more. He wonders if he should put in the time by familiarising himself with the controls of the car. He removes the instruction manual from the glove compartment and begins to riffle through, but quickly claps it shut again. He feels too tired suddenly for all this jargon and, besides, he is afraid of missing even one semi-second in the sighting of Sarla.

He looks down the road to the house that used to be his, one from the corner. The door still bears the same brass knocker that his mother brought from India, that time of the elongated visit. The knocker had been a family heirloom, or so his mother had claimed, although Ashok couldn't recall ever having seen it before. An elephant's head, intended to ward off evil spirits, it had an almost vicious expression on its face. His wife hadn't wanted such a blemish on their bright new door, although his mother had pretended not to understand this. Every evening when he returned from work she had been waiting on the doorstep in her widow's white sari, the elephant knocker in one hand and a hammer in the other, holding both out to him, smiling and nodding in that manic way he recognised from his boyhood. The smile that said, 'You wait till I get you home, my boy, you wait till I get you away from the prying eyes of strangers.'

Ashok finds it interesting to note that not only is the elephant still snarling there, but the door is the same cardinal red he had painted it the first summer they'd moved in, just after Sarla was born. He had taken such time in the painting of it, coat after careful coat, and how well it had lasted, considering. Still fresh by the time of the elongated visit – Sarla had been seven then. Not so fresh now, of course.

'Stupid old superstitious woman,' he mutters to himself, 'bloody cause of half the trouble.'

He reaches into his pocket and pulls out a fistful of charms: Hanuman, the monkey god with his garland of plastic flowers, next a small bunch of red chillis and finally Lord Ganesha himself. Looping them through the stalk of the rear-view mirror, Ashok watches them turn then settle. He stretches his fingers then presses the palms of his hands together and bows his head over the steering wheel. He prays that he may see Sarla, perhaps even find a chance to speak with her without the interference of her mother or a misguided nosey neighbour. He prays that he may make a good tip from today's cushy number to put towards the surprise for Sarla's birthday. He prays that his journey may be a safe one. That he may have peace in his mind, heart, and hands.

*

Sarla! She comes out of the house and lifts her face to the morning. Such a beautiful child, Ashok feels almost in awe of her. Even since yesterday, he sees changes that he can't quite name. And yet there are some things that have remained and will always remain. This pleases him no end: there is so very much about his daughter – hair, teeth, eyes, skin – that is Indian, and therefore undeniably his.

She stands for a moment blinking at the light and he wonders if the word 'sundust' is rising in her mind – a word that he gave to her, a long time ago. Just before the garden gate, she leans to settle one white sock then the other, even though both sit already snug to her smooth brown legs – and he knows she is listening to whatever row is taking place in the Carey house next door, where most mornings the four Carey wildcats scream and beat at each other. Recalling former rows – a schoolbag, a sandwich, a missing runner or a pair of knickers borrowed then returned, dirty, to a drawer – he wonders what today's topic could be and where it is taking place. He studies the turn of his daughter's head, one neat black plait glistening eel-like over one shoulder, and decides it must be the hallway.

He imagines the shadow theatre Sarla is now watching through the warp of glass in the porch windows. He tries to hear, as she is hearing, the screeches cartoonishly mingled. The swearing will be out of this world, he knows, particularly from the eldest girl, Jane, who seems to have been born with an angry tongue in her head.

Ashok remembers when Sarla was younger how these rows frightened her so. She used to think someone would be killed in there or that the wall would break under the strain of all that noise and violence, perhaps even fall on her head. He is pleased to see no fear now in the way she steps out onto the pavement, one hand smoothly closing the gate behind her.

He continues to watch as she balances her schoolbag on the narrow wall and begins fiddling with its strap. Now twisting her head for a peep down the road along the row of cars under the trees. He follows her eye as it trawls for a taxi sign then for the familiar silver of his Mondeo, before stopping and retracing and finally coming back to her schoolbag. Ashok knows she will not associate him with the sleek black shape in the middle of the row, that she will presume he hasn't turned up today. He knows, too, that this will make her at once relieved and disappointed. In his chest he feels his heart crack with the weight and pain of his love.

The car slips away from the kerb, secretive and smooth as a panther, so that Ashok is hardly aware that it's moved at all. He means for it to hold back, to give Sarla at least enough time to cross over the road and pass in through the school gate. But the Mercedes E-Class has a mind of its own as it prowls around the corner, only whispering to a stop a yard or so behind Sarla.

Ashok sits still. He watches his daughter, turning to cross over the road, glance at the car, glance again, then stop.

She takes a third, longer look over the rise of the bonnet, up the front windscreen, past Ganesha, and Hanuman, the bunch of dangling chillies, straight into her father's eyes.

A blush crawls up her cheeks as she returns to the pavement and comes around to the passenger door, her schoolbag held to her chest. Ashok finds the right button: in a moment the glass from the window has dissolved. He leans and shouts through it, 'Hi there, Sar-la!', as if it's the biggest surprise in the world to find her here.

Her eyes shift from side to side.

He continues, 'So how are you today? And, more to the point, how do you like my new car? Of course it's not really mine, only joking – well, it is mine, of course, I mean I didn't steal it or anything, but mine only for today. Work, you know. In a few moments I go to pick up someone from the airport. Do you know, Sarla-beti, what is meant by the phrase "cushy number"?'

He waits but she does not answer.

Ashok pats the passenger seat with one hand, with the other rubs his neck. 'Sarla, I have to tell you, quite honestly, my neck cannot take much more of this craning – come, come, sit in.'

She takes a step up to the car and looks in through the passenger window.

'You are like a picture there, in the frame of that window,' he says, drawing a square with his finger. 'You are truly more beautiful every day that I see you.'

'You're not supposed to be here, Dad,' she says. 'You're not supposed to …'

Ashok tries a shrug. 'I know,' he says, and then gives a small laugh.

'You'll get in big trouble.'

'You won't tell on your old papa-ji. Eh?'

'No. But I'll be late for school. I better, you know …'
She begins moving away.

'Sarla!' He shouts out her name and it sounds like a
plea for mercy. Ashok covers his mouth with his hand.

She steps back to the passenger door. 'Shhh,' she says,
her eyes shifting about again.

'Oh, yes, I'm so sorry. But Sarla-baby, things, you
know, things are really, really changing fast. You will not
believe how much.'

He lifts one hand and rolls his eyes in amazement,
then laughs again. 'You will see, oh, you will see.'

Sarla looks away from him. 'I really have to …' she
says, nodding her head towards the school.

He senses her slipping away. 'Yes. Yes, of course, but
first just let me quickly show you something.' He reaches
into his inside pocket. 'I shouldn't be doing this, I really
should not, but what the hell! This was to be your surprise
for your birthday – "The Ultimate Birthday Surprise!" –
see, it says so, here on the envelope. And I shouldn't say
anything until all is settled with your mother, but –'

'Dad, please …?'

'No, no, it will only take a moment, you wait, you see.'

He pulls out of the envelope two airline tickets and
flaps them at her.

'What's that?'

'What's that? What …? Only your ticket to India, Your
Highness. Our tickets, I should say. That's right, Sarla, your
father is taking you to India. To see your grandmother in
Bombay. Or Mumbai as I suppose we must now call it. And

all your relatives, so many cousins! All dying to meet the famous Sarla. Is it not truly the Ultimate Birthday Surprise? Can you imagine any better? You see – your father does keep his promises after all. Isn't it true? Say that it is so.'

Sarla says nothing.

'I can see that you are shocked,' he continues, 'naturally you are, after all it is not every day that a girl is given such a gift. Now, I don't want you to go worrying about your mother. I mean to say, how can she in all honesty refuse her only child this opportunity? What sort of a – what sort of a mother would she be? Six weeks, Sarla, and during the school holidays, so there can be no objection on educational grounds. I have been the greatest of misers, you know. I have the tickets and now I am working on our spending fund – we shall be like the Maharaja and his beautiful daughter. And we don't have to stay in Bombay. Oh no, we can travel elsewhere. India is such a – such a – vastness, you know. We can go on a train, maybe, or a boat or, Sarla, what about an elephant? We can go riding on an elephant. Talk about high-living! If you like, we needn't ever come back – oh no, only joking there. We will come back, of course. I've been saving so hard for this trip, so –'

Sarla bites down on her lip and her colour, which a moment ago had been so high, now fades to a sickly hue.

'I thought you were supposed to be saving for a new flat?' she says.

'Saving for a –?' He snorts out a laugh. 'Oh, really now, such an old head on young shoulders. All that will come. In the future come. But your poor old Naani, she doesn't have much future left. And she loves you so much. What fun you had when she came that time of the elongated visit. Do you remember? What fun!'

'Oh, for God's sake, Dad!'

'What? What?'

'Nothing.'

'Tell me, Sarla. You know that I only ask that you be honest with me. Tell me.'

'She's … you know? She's just –'

'What, for goodness sake? What?'

'That day, Dad! How could you forget that day?'

'That day?'

'With the Careys? Next door?'

Ashok lowers his eyes for a moment. 'Oh, yes. Oh, yes, I see.'

'I have to go now,' Sarla says.

He looks at her again. 'But, Sarla, that was only one day. Out of so many. And what harm really did she do when all was said and done? Your grandmother just doesn't understand the Western way and … I mean to say – the Careys? All right, all right, she shouldn't have, I know. But we needn't stay long in Bombay. Just hello, goodbye. Then we can –'

Ashok leans further towards the passenger door. He pushes the tickets towards her. 'Look now. Look! There is your name. There is your name written just there, in case you don't believe me. Don't ask me if you may keep the tickets please to show off to your friends. I implore you because I would only have to say no and how I hate to refuse my princess anything. Be patient – when all is settled with your mother you will realise the gift I am giving. Oh, and listen, I am finding a new lawyer. A better one. More expensive but, you know I always say, you pay for what you get in this life, Sarla. You really do. Here, go on, take a little peek. You know you want to …'

Sarla keeps her hands low. She looks to the sky and her eyes blister with tears.

'Oh, Sarla, you are overcome. Sit in the car, my bloody neck is really starting to kill me now. Come, sit with your father a moment.'

'I don't want to,' she says. 'I'm sorry, Dad. I am.'

'If you don't want to sit, that's all right, Sarla-baby.'

'No. I don't want to go. I don't want to *go*.'

She gives her head a vigorous shake and the tears fall out of it.

'You don't want to go to school? Is that what you mean?'

'I don't want to go to bloody India!' she cries, and then she is gone.

And he can't remember seeing her leave the window or cross in front of the car or go over the road. Yet there she is, a semi-second sighting of her at the gate of the school, just before she slips through a yielding wall of cabbage-green uniforms.

'Sarla!'

*

He nearly misses his VIP. His concentration wavering on and off Sarla and the traffic so dense, the parking elusive – every time he approaches what he believes to be a free space he finds some little bastard Mini or Fiat cowering at the back of it. What with one thing and another and all excuses aside, he left the bloody 'DeLuxe Chauffeuring

Welcome's Mr J. P. Ridell to Dublin!!' sign in the car and only thinks of it at all as he hurries through the arrivals hall and spots the other drivers already at the barrier, at ease and chatting amongst themselves, signs held loosely in their hands. Any minute now he knows they will stiffen like soldiers and their signs will go up like shields. To add to the matter, he finds he has also forgotten his mobile phone. This means, should any problem occur, he can't even contact Burke. He glances at the monitor. Flight DL102 already landed. Too bloody late now, anyhow.

Ashok edges in close to the barrier.

Beside him three older drivers, one in uniform, the other two in mufti, are moaning and groaning their way through a conversation. Any other time Ashook might have liked to join in, ask a question or put forth some observation of his own. But he feels as if he's been vacated somehow: his voice, his will, his sense of humour. Everything has gone through the school gates with Sarla.

He had forgotten all about the incident with the next-door Careys. Or 'The Final Straw' as his wife had come to call it. His fault, really, for not keeping an eye on things. But then again, how was he to know his mother would do such a thing? His wife really had no business blaming him – and Sarla? Sarla had no right to bring it up again this morning.

'My children were frightened,' Mrs Carey had said standing on the doorstep, a smug gleam of complaint in her eyes, 'frightened out of their wits, so they were.'

'That lot – frightened!' he had scoffed, more in defence than anything else. 'It is they should be made apologise. Not my mother, nor me.'

'Now you listen here to me,' she hissed, 'I don't know how you do things wherever the fuck it is you and that mad oul one comes from but in this country it's against the bleedin' law to break into somebody's house.'

'Break in! The back door is always open. And she only went in to clean your house as a neighbourly gesture. You should be grateful, kitchen spick-span for once in its life, windows gleaming, ironing all done. I really can't see the complaint, to be quite frank.'

'She tress-fuckin'-passed!'

'Mrs Carey, I don't appreciate your vulgar language in front of my daughter and my mother. And, and of course my wife. And if you kept your house more like a home and less like a pig sty then perhaps my mother would not have …'

The final straw. The final excuse, more like, to boot his poor mother out.

Ashok watches the traffic of passengers coming through the automated glass doors, the doors now and then giving a frustrated jolt, as if hoping in vain for a chance to close against the constant flow of human disruption. The area behind the barrier sluggish with movement. Ashok notices suitcases, attaché cases, haversacks, trolleys. He sees shoes, runners, boots, sandals and moccasins. When he begins to notice only faces, he knows the long-haulers are coming through. Tired, pasty faces looking as if they've been robbed of something. Time, he supposes.

His eye frisks the crowd. He dismisses women holding layers of Manhattan shopping bags, young men bent under rucksacks, a fat, red-faced family stuffed into Disneyland jerseys, an old lady carrying a yellow handbag.

He keeps his sights only on potential VIP material and reminds himself that if he is looking for Mr Ridell then Mr Ridell is also searching for him. They will know each other. He is certain of it.

The VIPs begin to stand out more clearly: a tall man with a buff mackintosh crooked over-arm; a navy-blue suit weaving through the rink, mobile phone nestled into his ear; an older man dressed in the uniform of an American academic – corduroy trousers, roll-neck, Hush Puppies shoes – all of whom pause as they come to the barrier and cast about for their names. Ashok is hopeful that he will be chosen. But one by one, each VIP locates his name and disappears with a driver, leaving only the usual humdrummerie behind (Welcome to Dublin. Enjoy your flight? Thank you, I did. If you just come this way? Thank you, I will). Then the next lot of drivers and greeters begin to arrive.

He tucks his chauffeur hat under his arm and makes his way to the customer desk.

He tries not to picture himself standing there with his shamed hot face and his eyes, animal-anxious, searching for his VIP. He tries not to hear the announcer's magnified voice dragging, without mercy, the name of Mr J. P. Ridell around the terminal walls. Or imagine what Burke is going to say when he finds out he has botched his cushy number. Most of all, he tries not to feel the clam of his shirt cloth against the sweat of his skin.

'Looking for Ridell?' a voice says somewhere, pronouncing it 'Riddle'. Ashok starts then turns round. An old woman with a square yellow handbag is standing behind him.

'That is quite correct. I'm waiting for Mr J. P. Ridell,' he says somewhat stiffly while at the same time taking the precaution of making a slight adjustment to the pronunciation.

'You're in for a long wait – he's been dead twenty years.'

Ashok blinks and says, 'Oh. I am so very sorry.'

'I guess I'm about over it now,' the woman replies. 'I'm Mrs Ridell. Mrs J. P.?'

He continues to stare. She has thick coiffed hair, stiff and white as meringue. Her face is beaky, eyes bright and a turquoise sort of blue. She is small and rather slight, yet still capable of carrying her well-cut clothes. Her hand, through the loop of her yellow handbag, is thin and freckled with age spots, her nails manicured and pearly pink.

'Why, yes. Yes, of course,' he hears himself bleat. 'You are the Missus, not Mister – they have made a mistake at the office. I am so very sorry. Welcome to Dublin,' he adds, diving straight into the pleasantries, 'I hope you had a pleasant flight. First time here? The weather has been most –'

'You don't have a sign. I'm supposed to look for a sign?'

'Yes, Ma'am. I do apologise. But if you care to tell me where your luggage –'

'Got any ID?' she asks him then.

'ID, Ma'am?'

'You know – identification, something to prove you are who you say? Something to prove you're my chauffeur?'

Ashok waits a moment before sheepishly taking his hat from under his arm. 'I have a hat,' he offers.

'He has a hat,' the woman repeats as if for the benefit of a third party. 'You know, anyone can have one of those?'

'Indeed, Ma'am.'

'Oh, what the heck,' she says, slapping the air with her fingers. 'What's the worst he can do – strangle me?'

'Really, Madam,' Ashok begins to protest, but she is already trotting ahead of him towards the exit door.

'My baggage is over here. I need to smoke. Now why don't you show me where I can do that while you go get the car?'

As soon as he gets back into the Mercedes, he checks his mobile phone. One message received. 'Sarla!' he says. 'Sarla. I knew you would come round.' But the message turns out to be from Burke.

'U Got Him Yet?'

'Her,' Ashok snaps at the phone. 'It's a bloody woman, you dough-faced fool.'

*

He settles Mrs Ridell into the back of the car. Before driving he twists in his seat to show her the 'Welcome Mr Ridell' sign. 'You see, Ma'am – how it says here Mister? But see now –' Ashok turns away from her, takes a pen from his pocket and carefully writes the letter S beside the Mr.

He comes back with the sign. 'Now we are all clear. I know who you are, and you know who I am.'

'Right,' she says as if she couldn't care less. 'He knows who I am, I know who he is.'

Then she sits back into the seat. 'But do you know a house by the name of Farmleigh?'

'If you mean the large house by the Phoenix Park, Ma'am, then indeed I do. Only last week, in fact, I took a government minister to that very house.'

'Good. So could you please take me there? And if we could drive through the Phoenix Park, I'd like to see it again, stop, stretch my legs, maybe.'

'Would you like to go now, Ma'am, or would you prefer to go first to your hotel to freshen up?'

'Do I look like I need freshening up?'

'Oh no, Ma'am. You look quite fresh enough already.'

She widens her eyes.

'What I mean to say, Ma'am, is not that you look fresh but –'

'So I don't look fresh enough?'

'Oh, you do, Ma'am, but –'

'So how do I look then? Go ahead, be honest, say the first thing that comes into your head.'

Ashok can hear the gulp in his throat.

'Like a lady, Ma'am.'

'Like a lady, he says.' Mrs Ridell laughs and sits back into her seat. 'I'm sorry – what's your name again?'

'Ashok.'

'I'm sorry, Ashok, I'm just kidding.'

'That's quite all right, Ma'am. I too enjoy a little joke from time to time.'

They leave the airport and on to the carriageway, where he sees through the rear-view mirror Mrs Ridell fussing through various items in her square yellow handbag. She looks like a child back there, so small and well-behaved, surrounded by a big bank of leather. Like Sarla once was. Except Mrs Ridell isn't a child. She is a small adult with an old face. And a big yellow handbag.

He wonders what to do with her now. To make conversation or wait to be spoken to? To run through the itinerary or await instructions? Or to throw a few 'touristy snippets' over his shoulder, as Burke has advised him to do in times of tight silences. But the silence is not tight, and Mrs Ridell seems most content to continue playing with her handbag.

Ashok is well used to women in his taxicab, but a female VIP in a chauffeured Mercedes is quite a different matter. There could be a long day ahead, just the two of them together, and she seems a little strange – the joke about him strangling her for example, and the way she sometimes appears to address a third person, as if there is a ghost in the car with them.

He thinks of Uncle Ravi, for years a driver for a tour company until an incident in the Rajahstan region – never to be spoken of again – got him the sack. From then on Ravi had worked as a chilli sorter, although his former glory days as a driver had made him the local expert on all matters foreign. Squatting in the doorway of the chilli store, knees level with his big bracket ears, red-stained fingers lazily mingling with the chillis, often seeming to melt right into them in fact. 'Lady People' is how Uncle Rav had referred to female passengers like Mrs J. P. Ridell. 'They are a different breed altogether. They need more attention – you know? You must address them often, and always as Ma'am. You must constantly check if they are comfortable and this above all else – if they need toilet facilities, remember they don't care for squats, only thrones for my lady. And somewhere with paper to wipe their little gandus – otherwise it will be the sulk-sulks for the remainder of the day. And they can't tell you why, and you can't ask them either. Because it's all guesswork when it comes to the "Lady People".'

The car is driving through the brick and foliage slope of the Drumcondra Road when he notices Mrs Ridell lift her small head to look out the window.

'Ma'am?' he asks.

'Yes, Ashok?'

'Comfortable, Ma'am?'

'Thank you, I am – how about yourself?'

'Myself, Ma'am?'

'That's right. You comfortable?'

'Oh! I'm comfortable also.'

'Even in that hat?'

'Ma'am?'

'You can take it off, you know. It's pretty warm today and really there is no need to wear it on my account.'

'Thank you, Ma'am, but I will leave it where it is for the moment.'

'Suit yourself. Might we have some air conditioning?'

'Certainly, Ma'am,' Ashok says and begins searching for the controls.

The traffic slows up into Dorset Street and he watches her turn the yellow handbag and press it down on her lap. From a pile she has made on the seat beside her, she takes

a writing pad and pen. Leaning on the handbag, she begins
to write.

'Ashok?'

'Ma'am?'

'I think you'll find that's the heating you've put on
there,' she says.

'Oh, excuse me, Ma'am!' Ashok gives a little laugh.
'Indeed it is.'

He adjust the controls – this time a blast of cold air
hurls out and Ashok hears himself gasp.

'A little extreme, don't you think?' Mrs Ridell says.

Ashok manages to switch off the blast.

Mrs Ridell looks up for a moment. ' Look, why don't
we just forget the air conditioning and open a window? Let
the real thing in, eh?'

'Yes, of course. And perhaps, after all, I will remove
my hat – if you are certain you don't mind, Ma'am.'

Ashok lays the hat on the seat beside him. Somewhat
alarmed by the sweaty glimpse of his flattened hair through
the mirror, he passes a surreptitious hand over his crown.

He glances at the car clock. It is three minutes to
eleven. Soon Sarla will be on her morning break and
will likely give him a call. He wonders should he perhaps
mention it in advance to his VIP?

He considers which why to put it. 'My daughter, you
know, we had a little misunderstanding this morning. I
hope you don't mind if I take that call? Children at that
age, you know how it is. She has just entered her teens and
I don't want her upset all the day long.'

He draws up at the traffic lights and is about to speak
when Mrs Ridell's little frosted head pops over the seat. She

is holding a page between her pearly nails. 'The itinerary – if you care to look it over?'

Ashok glances down through the list until the lights change and he has to move off again. The Phoenix Park remains in his head; the American ambassador's residence; Myo's pub, Farmleigh House and something about a race-course. At the next set of lights, he stops again, glancing this time to the end of the list. The Bailey pub and finally the Shelbourne Hotel for seven-thirty.

'You see, Ashok –'

'Yes, Ma'am?'

'I reckon I'll be about ready to sleep by eight-thirty this evening. I go to bed most nights at nine-thirty anyhow. So. Well, I thought, why not put in the day with a ride down Memory Lane?'

'Oh yes, Ma'am, indeed. It's a lane we all enjoy riding down from time to time.'

He looks at his mobile phone then back at the clock. Ten minutes past eleven. In five minutes Sarla's morning break will be over. Perhaps he should call her instead?

'Oh, by the way, Ashok, the Four Courts – if we could stop by?'

'You wish to go to the Four Courts, Ma'am?'

'Just for a peek. From the far side of the river – I can see it better there.'

'Oh, yes, Ma'am, indeed.'

Ashok veers the car to the left, forking down into Capel Street. The clock passes the quarter mark. 'Comfortable, Ma'm?' Ashok asks.

'No change there, Ashok.'

184

They cross over Capel Street Bridge and turn up
Essex Quay. A soft drift of river air through the half-
opened window. Across the way, The Four Courts, solid
and sunlit behind a fluster of leaves from the trees at
Arran Quay wall. 'Where's the stink gone?' she asks, and
Ashok feels a moment of alarm.

'The stink, Ma'am?'

'You know – the stink. This river used to stink like
hell.'

'Oh, that stink, Ma'am. Well – I don't really know. '

Mrs Ridell edges over to the quayside window. She
opens it fully as Ashok takes the car into a space by the
river wall. 'Would you care to get out for a moment? If
you have a camera I could take a nice snap of you?'

But she already has a pack of photographs in her
hand. He watches through the mirror, a blur of black-
and-white images slip one behind the other until one is
finally chosen. It looks like an old photograph of the
Four Courts. Mrs Ridell, her head dipping up and down
from the photo to the subject, appears to be verifying
something, or perhaps, Ashok thinks, even looking
for changes.

'All right, thank you. Drive on,' she says with an
absent-minded pat of her hand on the back of his seat,
and he knows then she is used to having a chauffeur.

Ashok turns the nose of the car in to the Phoenix Park.
On Chesterfield Avenue he says, 'Ma'am, you will notice
here the tea rooms. Over there the cricket ground, in a
moment the polo grounds. It is not unlike India in this
respect. The colonial connection, of course, and –'

'Yes, that's fine,' she says.

He decides to abandon the touristy snippets.

At the ambassador's residence she asks him to pull over. Ashok helps her out of the car and watches her move towards the entrance gate. Once more, she begins to sift through her pack of photographs. She turns to him then waves and points to her wristwatch to indicate that she won't be long. He sits and watches her disappear round the side of the ambassador's residence. Ashok picks up his mobile and sends a message to Sarla. She will be in class, but he knows these little scamps, they are always sending texts to each other, never minding the rules.

'Sarla hope u better mood? x Dad.'

He puts the message through, checks the report that says it's been delivered and waits. Through the mirror his eye falls on the yellow bag on the back seat of the car.

Mrs Ridell is gone so long Ashok begins to worry. He gets out of the car and looks around. Then he walks to the tunnel of trees that runs alongside Chesterfield Avenue and stands peering into its maw. In the gauze of green light he sees walkers, joggers, a dog zigaggedly sniffing. He steps over to the parallel tarmacadam lane and again looks up and down. A distant roller skater moving pendulously against an archway of sky, a woman walking like an overwrought puppet. And a little girl on a tricycle, a man trotting just behind her holding onto the saddle with one hand – a sight that seems to squeeze the blood out of his heart.

He gets back into the car and sends another message to Sarla.

'Sarla-ji please text all is ok to your father.'

The report states the message is pending. Ashok can hardly believe it – has she turned off her mobile phone? He calls the number and is put straight into message minder.

His first reaction is anger. She is cutting him, just like her mother has cut him so many times in the past. Switching off the phone. Locking all doors. After all the pinchfisting and doing without. All the looking forward to – no, *more* than that – all the living for the moment when he would hand her those airline tickets. And look how she had reacted to that! And now this cold-shouldering – is this how he is to be repaid for all his love and hard work!

'OK b that way U will b sorry now. Am finished with you. Forever.'

Ashok looks at the text he has written and feels a small, warm tingle of satisfaction. He continues: 'Jus like yr bloody mother.'

He feels better again and adds: 'yr bloody whore mother. Selfish bitch. U prob not even mine. Many other Asian drivers besides me in that cab company when she was telephonist.'

He immediately regrets and is ashamed of his message, even if he never had any intention of sending it. Poor little Sarla. After all, she is just a child and confused. Also it is quite possible that her teacher has confiscated the phone. Sarla would never be so cruel as to ignore him. He lifts his finger to the delete button, but a rap on the back window startles him and when he looks at the phone again he sees 'message sent' gliding across the screen. 'Oh no,' he groans, 'what have I done? I have pressed the wrong bugger.'

He jumps out of the car and opens the door for Mrs Ridell.

'You say something?' she asks him.

'Oh no, Ma'am. Nothing, I said nothing at all.'

Ashok's hands are slightly weak as he gets back into the driver's seat. He clutches the rim of the steering wheel.

'Comfortable, Ma'am?' he says.

'Look, why don't we agree on something? When I'm no longer comfortable, I'll let you know – OK?'

'Yes, Ma'am,' Ashok says.

'Excuse me, Ashok. I guess I'm a little tired.'

'That's perfectly understandable, Ma'am.'

'Anyhow, let's try for Farmleigh. You know how to get to ...?'

'Oh yes, Ma'am. In fact, only last week I took a government minister there.'

'So you said.'

The gates of Farmleigh are firmly shut. Mrs Ridell stands with her nose to the bars until a security guard appears. There are strings of wet grass and muck on the heels of her shoes, Ashok notices. The security guard tells her, then tells her again: the house is closed to the public except for certain days and this is not one of them. He is a fat chap, his belly arranged on a descending hill of three cushions pushing against the sky blue of his shirt. But Mrs Ridell will not be told. 'I'll be no trouble. I just need to see it again. It won't take more than ten minutes, tops. Okay, five. Five little minutes.'

'I'm sorry. I just can't.' He looks over her head at Ashok. 'I can't.' He shrugs and gives an apologetic grimace.

'What are you telling him for?' Mrs Ridell says. 'He's just the driver.'

Ashok, returning the grimace, smiles broadly at the security man. 'Just the driver,' he confirms.

'Oh, come on now,' Mrs Ridell says, 'surely you can help me out here? What difference is five minutes going to make to your life? Five lousy minutes. Am I being unreasonable here? Am I asking too much? Five minutes – is that such a big deal for an old woman at the end of her days?' She draws her hand around in a semi-circle as if appealing to a jury only she can see.

'Sorry,' the security guard says.

She speaks to Ashok from the side of her mouth. 'Could you bring my purse from the car, please?'

Ashok returns with the bag.

'I can pay you for your trouble,' Mrs Ridell says to the security man, snapping her fingers at the bag. 'I mean, if it comes to that.'

Ashok steps forward and holds the bag out to her. But Mrs Ridell doesn't take it. Instead, she shoves her two thin arms through the rails of the gate, pulls one photograph out of her bundle and thrusts it at the security guard.

'Look, I was a guest here a long time ago. See? That's me. Right there.'

Ashok strains to make out the frame of a large house, people sitting outside it, a conservatory, a lawn. He can't see the woman who used to be Mrs Ridell because the pink-pearly nail of the present Mrs Ridell is blocking his view. The security guard won't look at the picture. Now he begins to back away, raising his hands as if he is vaguely expecting Mrs Ridell to draw out a gun. 'Lookit. Even if I wanted to, I couldn't. There's an important meeting on here today. Government biz. Can't let you in. You know yourself.'

'You know yourself? You know yourself?' Mrs Riddell asks. 'What in hell's that supposed to mean?'

He walks away up the avenue. She stands for a while looking after him, a fan of photographs still in her hand. Ashok stands beside her, the yellow handbag looped over his arm. He can't get over the security guard, how thin he looks from behind, like another man in fact.

Mrs Ridell gets back into the car; the photographs slide from her hand down onto the seat. Ashok cautiously places the handbag beside her.

'How disappointing,' she says, looking out the far window. 'Oh, how very, very disappointing.'

'I am sorry, Ma'am, I thought you knew it was no longer a private house.'

'Oh, for goodness sake, how could I know that!'

He is about to drive off when the mobile sounds, then sounds again. He checks and sees both his messages to Sarla have just gone through.

'Ma'am?' he begins, turning to look over the back seat. 'I wonder, Ma'am, if I might take a moment to send a message on my mobile telephone? It is a matter of some urg–'

'Sure, go ahead,' Mrs Ridell says with some impatience.

'Sarla – so v. sorry for last message. Sent in error. Please forgive. Love from so sorry dad.'

'So,' Mrs Ridell sighs, 'the racecourse, I guess.'

'The racecourse, Ma'am?'

'That's right. The Phoenix Park racecourse. Tell you what, let me see if I can remember how to find it. OK, take a left here, down this road, past the school, back into the park.'

'Yes, Ma'm,' Ashok says and begins following her directions.

Just before Ashtown Gate she asks him to pull to the kerb.

'Ah yes, Ma'am,' he says. 'I believe I know where you mean. But you do realise –?'

She has the door open before he has a chance to tell her. Ashok slips his mobile phone into his pocket before hurrying around to help her out of the car. Then she trots ahead of him through Ashtown Gate onto Blackhorse Avenue, where he catches up with her at the kerb. She is staring across the road. Her hand is over her mouth and her eyes wide awake. 'Oh no! Oh my!' she says.

Ashok helps her to cross the road, holding her at the elbow with his free hand slowing a car that has come spinning around the corner.

They stand at the entrance to the former racecourse, the ground beneath their feet mutilated by heavy machinery, the air muffled with the churn and rattle of a half-constructed building site.

'I never thought,' she says, raising her voice to carry, 'I mean, I just never. Of all the – you know? The last thing I expected in Ireland – in Dublin – was to find a racecourse, well, obliterated, I guess. And for this? What is this anyhow?'

'Apartment living, I believe they call it, Ma'am. A development. Or something.'

'Or something, he says!' She gives him a look of disgust in return for his inadequate explanation. They begin to walk back to the kerb.

Ashok's phone, like a large bee in his pocket, buzzes.

'Oh, please don't mind me,' she snaps. 'Go on right ahead and take it.'

He pulls the phone out of his pocket and, turning one shoulder slightly, reads a message from Sarla.

'If u don't leav me alone I tell u follow me evry day. I tell Mam and she call police. BTW I hope am NOT yrs cos I rly rly HATE u.'

Mrs Ridell looks at his face as they cross back over the road. 'Everything all right?' she asks.

'Oh, absolutely perfectly so, Ma'am. Thank you for asking,' Ashok replies with a cheek-splitting smile.

At the park gate Mrs Ridell turns and takes one last look at the old racecourse entrance. 'You know what I could do with? I could do with a drink. Take me to Myo's – would you? Unless that's been converted to apartments too.'

*

Mrs Ridell comes out of Myo's, two bindi-like spots high on her cheekbones. Ashok takes her elbow and guides her in, closing the door on a dark, yeasty waft of overripe figs – in other words whiskey.

As he walks around the car he sees her tidying the photos back into the flap then into a zip compartment of the yellow handbag. He sits back in the car and now she is working on the little pile, earlier left spread across the seat, picking each item up then willy-nilly dropping it into the bag: pen, lipstick, hairbrush, writing pad, cigarettes. Ashok can't understand how such a well-groomed lady could be so disorganised.

'So – you get to finish making all your telephone calls?' she asks.

'Excuse me, Ma'am?'

'I was sitting by the window, and twice I came out for a cigarette – you were on the cell phone the whole time.'

'It was only one call, actually, and I couldn't get through. Well, at first there was no response then, later, the caller was not in range.'

'But you kept trying?'

'Yes. But now I'm finished trying.'

A moment passes.

'You know, I think I'm just about done in, Ashok. You may as well take me to the hotel now.'

'So soon?'

'I guess I'm a little tired.'

Ashok turns and looks at his VIP. A little more faded now, her head resting on the back of the seat, the soft leather yielding beneath it. There is a flat, weary look in her eyes.

'If you are sure there is nothing else?'

'No. That's fine – well, maybe one more thing. A question really.'

'Ma'am – please just ask it.'

'On my walk today, I went looking for the deer. But I couldn't find them. I didn't like to ask because, well, I guess, I was afraid you'd say they no longer keep deer in the Phoenix Park.'

'I can assure you they certainly do. The deer, you see, congregate in different areas depending on the time of day. I can take you to see them now, if you so wish?'

'You sure about that, Ashok? You sure you know where they are? Because, let me tell you, I don't need another let-down today.'

'Ma'am – I know that Phoenix Park like my own backyard!'

The car twists up along the Military Road past the Magazine Fort. Ashok considers turning into the first and smaller car park – a cosy green haven with a few parked cars, a single man to each one. But he has heard the salacious rumours of what sometimes goes on in there and doesn't want his VIP viewing more than the deer. He turns into the second, larger car park, where he brings the Mercedes to an angled stop. The playing fields on one side, stretching pitch after pitch into the deep green distance; on the other side the ugly grey block of the changing-rooms. To the front, the deer, arranged in quiet dun-coloured groups under the trees.

Mrs Ridell releases a sigh. 'They are so beautiful,' she says.

'Indeed, Ma'am.'

'They are so …?'

'Peaceful?' Ashok suggests, turning to see her small face peeping out between the seats.

'You know, Ma'am,' he continues, 'you would enjoy a clearer view were you to sit here in the front seat alongside me.'

Mrs Riddell bites her lip and gives a grateful, girlish nod.

Ashok removes his chauffeur's hat from the passenger seat and lays it on the dashboard then gets out of the car, comes round to the back door and helps her move into the front. The yellow handbag stays behind.

A light shower begins to fall, the windscreen gradually filling with a thin coating of rain. They sit silently watching the deer. After a time Mrs Ridell speaks. 'You know, I don't recall the grass being so long last time.'

'Oh and it will get longer, Ma'am. The fawning season, you see, which will soon begin. The grass is always longer during this time. Except for the playing fields, which of course must remain clipped.'

'I like it long – it looks, well, less contrived, I guess.'

'Or more natural, Ma'am.'

'Or that too.'

'It is really at its most beautiful at daybreak, and then again just before sunset. In these moments, the long grasses turn pink at the tips. With the red of the sky and the push of the breeze, it's like the grass is painting the sky – you know? It is quite the most extraordinary thing I've seen since I've been here. Well, that and the silent traffic jam – also extraordinary but in a different way.'

'How long have you been here, Ashok?'

'Me? Oh, about fifteen years.'

'You like it?'

'Oh yes, very much, Ma'am, thank you for asking. Well, no, actually, not really. At least, not so much as I used to.'

'Do you have family here?'

Ashok gives a little smile then turns his face to the side window. After a moment he speaks. 'If you were to get out of the car now and walk way out there to where the grass is longest, sooner or later you would hear the sound of a fawn crying. A most pitiful sound. And if you were to follow the sound you would find the poor creature all alone and huddled in the grass. The temptation, of course, would be to lift it up and carry it off to safety. But you must never do that.'

'No?'

'Oh no. No matter how much your heart may tell you to. You see, once you touch it, the mother would consider the fawn to be contaminated and then she would abandon it.'

'I see. How odd.'

'The laws of nature are not always easy to understand,' Ashok hears himself mutter.

'Ashok –?' she begins, but he stops her with a smile and a lift of his hand. 'Oh, Ma'am, excuse me rambling on when I really meant to ask if you would care to have a cigarette here, in the car? Seeing as how it is raining outside.'

'Why, thank you, Ashok. That would be wonderful. To have a cigarette sitting in comfort? I don't know when I last!'

He gets out of the car and pulls the handbag from the back seat.

'In your own home, Ma'am,' he says as he gets back into the car.

'Excuse me?'

'In your own home you must allow yourself to enjoy, in comfort, a cigarette.'

'Oh, yes, I see what you mean. But no. I don't have a home as such. I live in hotels mostly, since my husband died.'

Mrs Ridell opens the bag and rummages through the contents until she finds first a lighter then a pack of cigarettes. The cigarettes are jammed in together, her fingers tugging like a bird at a worm in an effort to release one. Up close her hands look older; her pearly-pink nails seem to hover rather than rest on her fingertips.

Ashok takes the pack from her hand. He pulls out a cigarette and gives it to her then holds the lighter up and clicks. A perfect drop of fire. Mrs Ridell pokes the tip of her cigarette into it and puffs. Ashok presses a button and her window purrs open.

'When I was a child,' he says, 'my mother had a yellow handbag.'

Mrs Riddell puts her head to one side as though inviting him to continue, but he waits until she has turned her face away from him and back towards the deer.

'Yes. A German lady gave it to her,' he says then. 'My mother, you see, she worked in the Taj Palace Hotel as a cleaner. The most beautiful hotel in Bombay – I don't know if you've been?'

'No. But I've heard of it, sure.'

'She was most fortunate to have such a job. One day when she was scrubbing the floor on one of the corridors a German lady going into her room dropped her key.

My mother picked it up and opened the door for the woman. As she went to hand back the key, she saw that the woman was weeping, sobbing in fact. So she opened the door herself and went into the room and stayed until the woman finally fell asleep. She never saw the woman again, although she did remain several more days as a guest in the hotel. Nor did my mother ever know what it was that had made her weep so. After the woman had checked out of the hotel, the head housekeeper came to my mother and handed her a brown-paper parcel. Inside was the yellow handbag. My mother had noticed it in the German lady's room and thought perhaps the lady had, in turn, noticed her admiring it.'

Ashok stops for a moment.

'Go on,' Mrs Ridell says, before twisting her head away and pushing a wisp of smoke out the window.

'There is nothing to go on with. Except … Well, when we were children, we thought she carried a piece of the sun around with her in that yellow handbag. Every time she opened it, something wondrous would emerge: small, fragrant soaps, pieces of individually wrapped chocolate, pens and writing paper too – oh, as thick as cloth. A stick of kohl for my sisters' eyes, a ribbon for their hair. Once a *Boy's Own* annual for me! Such luxury was unheard of in our lives, so it was easy to believe the source would have to be magical. I realise now, of course, that these things were stolen from the great Taj Hotel and that the sun had nothing to do with it.'

'But the yellow purse – that wasn't stolen.'

'No, Ma'am. But neither was it a true gift.'

'Oh, but surely …?'

'A true gift is given from one hand and is accepted by another. The German lady should have personally given it to my mother if she intended it as a gift.'

'What was it then?'

'I don't know, Ma'am. A mark of gratitude? A release of obligation? But my mother – she could never truly own it.'

Mrs Ridell tilts her chin towards the butt of her cigarette and takes one final pull before throwing it out the window. 'And your mother, Ashok? Is she still alive?'

'Oh yes, Ma'am. She is old. Very old. But alive and very well too, thank you. In India. With my brothers. My sisters, unfortunately, are no longer with us.'

'And you – have you no family? No children, no wife?'

Ashok slips the chauffeur's cap from the dashboard and begins to pick at its braided cord.

'I have no one, Ma'am. Only my mother and brothers in Bombay, or Mumbai, as I suppose we must call it now. I will be seeing them again in a few weeks' time.'

'Well now! I bet you're looking forward to that.'

'Oh yes, Ma'am. I suppose I am.'

'And will you return to Ireland? After your vacation, I mean.'

'Oh now, Ma'am,' he smiles, 'that is a very good question.'

Ashok steps out of the car, placing the chauffeur's hat back onto his head. 'We will go soon, Mrs Ridell,' he says, 'but if you would allow me a moment or two?'

'Of course, Ashok, you take as long as you like.'

He walks through flimsy rain across the cracks and bumps of the tarmacadam car park, coming to a stop at the edge where the grass is at its shortest. A lone grazer has strayed from the herd and is plucking its way out from the trees towards the wide-open space of the playing field. Ashok watches it for a while then slips his hand into his pocket. For a moment he hears the sounds of his childhood: boys' voices and the batting of cricket balls. Dipping at the knee, he sends his phone in a daisy-cutter bowl, across the grass towards the trees.